SHEPHERD'S SON

MYSTERIOUS WAYS SERIES

SHEPHERD'S SON

A NOVEL BY

Terry W. Burns

RIVEROAK®
Good News in Fiction

An Imprint of Cook Communications Ministries
COLORADO SPRINGS, COLORADO • PARIS, ONTARIO
KINGSWAY COMMUNICATIONS LTD
EASTBOURNE, ENGLAND

RiverOak® is an imprint of
Cook Communications Ministries, Colorado Springs, CO 80918
Cook Communications, Paris, Ontario
Kingsway Communications, Eastbourne, England

SHEPHERD'S SON

Published in association with Hartline Literary Agency, 123 Queenston
Drive, Pittsburgh, PA 15235.

This story is a work of fiction. All characters and events are the product of
the author's imagination. Any resemblance to any person, living or dead,
is coincidental.

Cover Design: Jeffrey P. Barnes
Cover Illustrator: Ron Adair

First Printing, 2006
Printed in the United States of America

        1 2 3 4 5 6 7 8 9 10 Printing/Year 10 09 08 07 06

All Scripture quotations are taken from the King James Version of the
Bible. (Public Domain.)

ISBN-13: 978-1-58919-033-7
ISBN-10: 1-58919-033-5

LCCN: 2006927928

Dedicated to our shepherd, Brother Leon Green, and his wife, Jeanette, and to our church family at Bolton Street Baptist Church in Amarillo, Texas

One

*T*he riders came over the hill riding low and fast, bandannas obscuring their faces. Some swung coiled ropes in their hands as they bore down on their prey in the valley.

Moments before it had been a pastoral scene, a sea of white sheep grazing peacefully across the lush green grass of the pasture. The only fence was the salt cedar bushes that surrounded it on the slopes, which gave way farther up the hill to evergreens and taller pines.

Jay Mendelson sat halfway up the slope and dozed as he trusted the flock to the watchful eye of the Border collie by his side. Equal to the task, Lady would leave his side without instructions to corral any errant sheep and send them scampering back to the safety of the flock.

Jay used his flat-crowned hat for a pillow, his straw-colored hair spilling into his eyes. It always resisted any efforts to curry or comb it. His green eyes cataloged the clouds with no conscious effort, and the good-natured smile that was more habit than anything else played gently across his face.

The spring day had been so lazy and peaceful, the air still fresh from a short morning shower, that it lulled him into a reverie. It caused him to be slow to respond, his brain not really believing what his eyes were trying to tell him.

Lady already knew they were coming, and as they topped the ridge she launched herself at the riders, leaping between the men and her charges. The man in the lead fired his pistol, and she went down.

Jay jumped for the old Winchester rifle leaning against his pack. He snatched it up and levered a shell into it as he spun. A rider was nearly on top of him as he brought it to his shoulder.

"Too late, boy," the man said.

The lights went out as the rider swept past, striking down with his pistol barrel. Jay went down hard. Somewhere in the back of his mind he heard the noises of the riders charging the flock: shooting, killing, scattering. He was powerless to do anything about it.

Blake Johnson, known to most as "the colonel," sat staring into the fire in the huge fireplace that anchored his study. Later in the day it would be quite comfortable, but here in the high country it was cool and crisp well into the mornings, continuing on into the summer months. He absentmindedly pulled on the cigar in his hand, alternating the puffs with sips from the huge cup of coffee by his side.

Johnson was a big man, but solid. His black hair showed gray at the temples, and his full mustache had already faded to a salt-and-pepper color. His piercing green eyes had been known to nail subordinates to the wall.

"We scattered them to the four winds, Colonel."

Johnson had not heard the man enter. Rafe Silbee seemed to have the uncanny ability to appear and disappear when he was needed or not required. As the First Sergeant in Johnson's regiment, the man had been invaluable to Johnson, and when Johnson mustered out to come west and establish a ranch, he had brought the man with him to serve as his foreman.

Any other man might have thought in terms of partnership, being in on the initial establishment of a ranch like the Circle J, but as a career military man, Silbee was used to taking orders and submitting to authority. He fit Johnson's needs perfectly.

The colonel didn't bother to look up. "You didn't hurt the boy?" It was more of a statement than a question.

Silbee stood at a rough semblance of attention. "Fetched him a clout up beside the head is all. Couldn't let him go shooting one of the men. Had to shoot the dog though."

"Too bad. I like dogs."

Silbee stood there, awaiting further orders. He was as tan as a saddle, lean and sinew tough, hair still cut army short, gray eyes always measuring, calculating. "It had to be done, sir."

A voice an octave higher entered the conversation, "What had to be done?"

Silbee jerked his hat from his head. "Morning, Miss Carrie Sue."

The colonel frowned. He didn't like to see his daughter wearing pants. Dressed to go for a ride, she was also wearing a man's shirt, boots, and a flat-crowned Stetson hat. Tethered by a string to hang down her back, the hat wouldn't come into play until she needed it. Her red hair was pulled back and tied with a bow, and the bright auburn color made her blue eyes all that more startling.

"Daddy, what is it that had to be done?" she repeated.

"Something you don't need to concern yourself about. You go for your ride; we have business to conduct." Her father's tone indicated she was dismissed.

The blue eyes blazed. Able to command a full regiment of troops with absolute confidence, the colonel was powerless against his daughter's eyes.

She put her hands on her hips and raised her voice. "Daddy!"

He resorted to his command voice. "Don't you try to intimidate me!"

Carrie Sue stared at her father with a look of determination, but not without kindness.

He let out a sigh. "You're just like your mother. She used to wheedle anything out of me she wanted." His voice softened. "God rest her soul, I couldn't deny her anything."

His daughter's eyes remained locked on his. He sighed again, deeper this time. "Just like her."

He looked back to Silbee for support, but the man was gone. Johnson wondered how he did that. He transferred his gaze to the fire and surrendered.

"I had to have the boys give a little object lesson to those sheepherders," he said quietly.

"Please tell me you're kidding. Those people aren't hurting you."

His tense voice revealed his indignation. "They brought sheep into cattle country. I can't allow that. You know sheep and cattle can't graze the same land. I can't allow it."

"So you sent your big, bad cowboys over to the Bar-M to terrorize a little widow lady? You know very well that Mrs. Mendelson ran cattle until her husband died. He was one of you."

His head turned, and his eyes met her challenge. "Exactly, Jack was one of us, and if he were still alive he'd be standing with me trying to keep sheep out of the valley."

"If he were alive, his wife wouldn't have had to bring in sheep, trying to make a living. She and Jay couldn't handle the cattle alone, and couldn't afford help, so they sold what was left to buy a flock of sheep that they could handle. I thought that was pretty smart."

He wasn't buying it. "There's nothing smart about introducing sheep into cattle country."

Two

J ay sat up, his vision blurred. It made it hard to focus on the scene before him. His head throbbed, and he put a hand up to gingerly test the goose egg high on his temple. He winced; not a good idea. Then he caught sight of Lady.

"Oh no."

He ran to kneel by the collie's side. She was moving, but each breath was shallow, labored. He picked her up gently. As he turned, he saw the valley floor littered with the bodies of sheep; the remainder of the flock was gone. He was needed, and needed badly, but first things had to be done first. He hurried to the ranch house with Lady in his arms.

He thought as he ran that the bandanna had done nothing to hide Silbee's military demeanor. Jay knew who the riders had been also. Silbee had called him "boy," and he had recognized the cold voice. It wasn't surprising he had called him that. The colonel usually did it as well, mostly because the colonel had watched Jay grow up with his daughter, seen them together in school. He didn't consider his daughter as grown either.

But Jay had been doing a man's work for years, particularly after his father had been killed in a fall trying to corral a wild steer. Taking over running the Bar-M ranch, carrying that load, had made him lean and well muscled, a man by anyone's standards.

Man or not, his eyes were moist as he rushed back to the house. Lady was his closest friend, and he couldn't work the flock without her. Silbee had probably known that, he thought. The man undoubtedly knew that was the way to make the greatest impact on them. Silbee was mean. No, that wasn't true. Meanness was an emotion, and Silbee had no emotion—good, bad, or otherwise. He was a military machine, logical and efficient, and emotion didn't enter into it.

Jay stumbled into the clearing where the small cabin, bunkhouse, and barn stood, surrounded by a variety of pens and corrals, an unusual mixture of each that testified to the conversion from cattle to sheep. The conversion had been his mother's idea, and even though the logic of what she had decided was immediately apparent to him, it hadn't felt right. He'd been raised the son of a cattleman, a cowboy, and his nature rebelled against what he was being asked to do. Still, taking care of his mother came first, and he saw no better alternative that would allow the place to pay for itself, to provide a living, than what she had asked him to do—switch to raising sheep.

He had been surprised to find himself drawn to the gentle creatures, so totally dependent on him, and on the dog that was their ramrod and their protector. That had been a surprise to him.

Audrey Mendelson came out on the porch as her son approached the house, wiping her hands on her apron as she moved to meet him. "What happened?"

Concern burned in her chocolate-colored eyes as Jay came toward her. Married and a mother by the time she was fifteen years old, she still had a girlish figure and looked more like Jay's sister than his mother.

"Masked riders rode down on the flock. I don't know why they bothered with the masks; it ain't like I wouldn't recognize Silbee when I saw him. It was him that banged me up beside the head."

She reached out to his wound. "Let me see that."

He shrugged her hand off. "He shot Lady. We got to see to her."

He brushed by her to carry the dog inside and lay her gingerly on the table. His mother poured some hot water from the stove into a pan and then came to the table with some cloth that had once been a sheet. She bent down to inspect Lady's side. Living so far from civilization, she had done her share of doctoring, and this was not the first bullet wound she had treated.

"Entry and exit wound. It passed though clean, no bullet to have to remove. Shoulder muscle; I don't think it hit anything vital. Your Mr. Silbee is not a very good shot."

"He ain't *my* Mr. Silbee, and he's a mighty good shot. I guess a dog coming at him in the air was just a really hard target."

"That or perhaps God played a hand in it."

Jay rubbed Lady's neck. The animal was completely oblivious to his touch, a blessing since she did not react as

Audrey cleaned the wound and dressed it. "You saying she's going to be all right?"

"She'll have a tough go of it for a while. We need to immobilize her somehow to keep her from moving until she heals, but I think she'll be all right. Can you go get me some tree moss to make a poultice to put on as I bandage the wound?"

Carrie Sue stomped out of her father's study in a huff. She loved him, but sometimes she did not understand him. For such a strong man, there were times she felt he was controlled by others and what they might think of him. When her mother was alive, she could diplomatically make gentle suggestions that would moderate his decisions. Not control him—she would have never done that—simply make comments that allowed him to think more clearly.

Carrie Sue wished she had inherited that ability from her mother. Her opposition often did nothing but cause her father to set his heels like a stubborn mule, and if she were honest, he often did the same to her.

The ranch blacksmith saw her leave the house, and he led out the little palomino he had saddled for her. She smiled her thanks and swung up into the saddle. She needed to think, and riding was her preferred method of doing just that.

She reined the golden horse with the flowing mane and tail in a tight circle, bent low over her neck, and left the yard at a gallop. The mare was tired of the confines of the stall and ready to run. This was just fine with her rider.

They ran for several miles, working out their frustration. Finally Carrie Sue pulled up, stepped down, and walked the horse to cool her down before she led her over to the sparkling little stream for a drink. When the horse had her fill, Carrie Sue allowed her to graze the tender grass beside the stream. She lay back on a big rock to think, and her thoughts went to Jay Mendelson.

She and Jay had been close in school, good friends. Only lately had she been considering the possibility that her feelings might go further. Her father would have probably been very receptive, until Jay had become a sheepherder. That was unforgivable in the rancher's mind.

Once Lady's wound was dressed, Audrey and Jay taped her front legs together so she could not move in any way that would pull the stitches apart. They made her a bed by the fire. She woke up and licked Jay's hand. He knew she didn't understand what had happened, didn't understand why her legs didn't move, but she did seem to accept that whatever they were doing, it was for her good.

Jay got up. "I've gotta go see about the flock."

His mother smiled. "You go ahead. Lady will be fine."

"I know."

"How will you handle them without her?"

Jay pulled on his hat. He went to the trunk that held the remains of his father's belongings and pulled the old Navy Colt six-shooter from it. "I'll need help. Paco Gonzales and his family are having it pretty tough right now; we might be able to help each other." He checked the bullets in the pistol, then belted it on.

Audrey didn't acknowledge the significance of her son belting on the pistol, but she knew what it meant. "We've no money to pay them."

"We got mutton, a pasture full of it. I'm gonna ask if his wife and girls will help me gather the flock, and I'll see if Paco and his boys will start butchering the dead sheep and smoking the meat. I'll give them the fleece and split the meat with them. I think they'll do it. That oughta be enough meat to last them for some time. Us too."

The pride was clear in her eyes. "That's good thinking."

"I hope so." He pulled open the door. "I got to hurry though, that meat won't last long once the day starts to heat up."

Jay rode into Three Forks, the nearest town, where he stopped at the small Gonzales house on the outskirts and made the deal. As he predicted, the family was glad for the chance. They loaded into a wagon and started to the task. He told them he would join them soon, but he had an errand to run first.

His errand took him to the saloon, but not to drink; that was something he had never done. He knew that after a raid Silbee would want to celebrate the victory. He expected him to be there, and he was. The big man stood, one foot on the rail, with a drink in front of him on the bar. Jay walked up behind him and tapped him on the shoulder.

Silbee paused, his drink just shy of his lips, and looked back over his shoulder. Jay hit him as hard as he could, stepping forward to put his entire weight behind the punch. It drove the shot glass into the man's face, breaking it on his teeth.

A yellowing tooth bounced across the floor like spare change lost from a pocket. Blood welled up on Silbee's lips. He rolled down the bar, keeping himself upright with his elbows. Jay stepped right behind him, spinning him again with two more solid punches.

With a guttural roar, Silbee tried to push off the bar to defend himself but lost his balance. He went down hard, ending up on his back. He looked up, wiped the blood from his mouth with the back of his hand, and looked at it in a disinterested manner. "You're making a big mistake."

"My dog ain't dead." Jay stood over him, feet spread, fists still balled.

"Too bad. I intended him to be."

Silbee's cool mind weighed the options. If he tried to get up, the boy was sure to kick him square in the face—at least that's what he would do if their positions were reversed. He didn't care what others in the bar might think. "I never figured you for a sneak attack."

Jay's face was still clouded with anger. "Like riding down on a defenseless flock of sheep with a lone man isn't a sneak attack? It's no sneak attack now though. Get up, and let's get to it."

"I ain't figuring on getting up with you standing over me. Back up a bit, and I'll oblige you."

Jay stood his ground. "I like it here. If you're not of a mind to show these people what you're made of, lemme tell you this. You shot a defenseless dog, and this is a little attention-getter to let you know that if you or anybody else ever takes *any* kind of further action against my dog, I'm gonna come take it out on you. If I have to have a board in my hands to give you a sufficient beating, I'll do it."

Silbee still made no effort to rise. "You think I'm gonna let this stand?"

"I hope not, I really do, but I want everybody in the room to hear this. If there's to be more, it'd better be between us, and not against some gentle dog that wouldn't hurt a fly."

He backed up a couple of steps. "And I'd just as soon it be now. I'm in the mood to do it. There's your space to get up. Let's see what you've got."

Silbee got up warily. "No, I don't think so. I don't like to dance to a tune when somebody else is paying the fiddler. I'll finish this, but I'll pick the time and the place." He bent over and picked up his hat.

Silbee wiped his mouth again, leaving a blood smear. He smirked. "I'll give you this much though. I don't think I'm gonna call you boy anymore. Those punches felt man-sized to me."

He walked past Jay and through the swinging door.

Three

*B*y the time Jay got back to the pasture, several fires were going, and meat was drying on racks made of green sticks. He could see the young girls and boys as they gathered sheep on the hillside, moving them back toward the pasture. Audrey came down the hillside on her way from the Bar-M, bringing a number of sheep with her. They had wasted no time.

He tied off his horse and headed up to help his mother. She noticed the look on his face, glanced down at his bleeding knuckles, and said, "Violence doesn't settle a thing."

"It's all a man like Silbee understands. I can't have him coming after Lady when she's back on her feet."

She saw no marks on his face and understood what that meant. "Did it work?"

"If he knows what's good for him."

She shook her head. "It's not over."

He was under no illusions about that. "It wasn't going to be over anyway. It has nothing to do with the dog, and I figure I made that clear to everybody in town. Now if people hear of something happening to her, they'll think mighty small of him. He's smart enough to know that; but you're right, it ain't over about the sheep, not by a long shot."

"Maybe I should just sell them."

Jay shook his head vigorously. "You do, and the Bar-M is gone. I can support us. I can get a riding job where I can make enough money to care for us, but if I do that we'll lose the place. I know you don't want that, and neither do I."

Jay's eyes swept up to the ridgeline. "He didn't waste any time."

"What?" She turned to see several riders at the top of the ridge.

"Get Paco, Rosita, and the kids away from the flock," Jay said, "back in those trees. These guys ain't after you all."

Audrey's eyes reflected her fear. "What are you going to do?"

"What I have to do." His face was impassive. He was obviously resigned to the task at hand.

Jay walked toward the riders as they started down the slope. Audrey ran to Jay's horse, pulled the rifle from the scabbard, and then turned to follow him. Paco pulled an old shotgun from under the seat of his wagon and caught up with her.

Jay looked at them as they stepped beside him. "I told you two to go take care of Rosita and the kids."

Audrey's face was grim. "I think not."

Paco flashed a broad smile, revealing a missing a tooth in front. "You have been good to me and to my family, Señor Jay. These men, they have not."

The riders were down off the slope now, riding slowly across the pasture. Rifles pulled from scabbards were held in their hands. Hooves sounded behind him, and Jay swung around, drawing his pistol. It was Carrie Sue. She rode up next to the trio and stepped down from the saddle.

Jay shook his head. "You shouldn't be here."

The smile he received in return was dazzling. "Of course I should."

The riders pulled up. Silbee glowered and echoed Jay's comment. "Carrie Sue, you shouldn't be here."

"Funny, that's what Jay just said. You do anything against these people, and you're going to have to do it to me too. You ready to explain that to Daddy?"

Silbee held up his hands as if warding off her words. "Just came to talk."

She was all rancher's daughter addressing a subordinate. "Bristling with guns like spikes on a porcupine? How stupid do you think I am?"

The hands dropped, "No, I-I-I only came to say I was sorry about his dog."

"You'd better be," she barked, "and nothing else better happen to that dog. I have no respect for a man who'd wage war against a defenseless animal."

"I told you it was an accident, but I figure you oughta go talk to your father about what he wants here. You know me, I just follow orders. I'm just a simple old soldier."

Her chin came up. "No, you'd best go make sure you are clear on what your orders are. And if I were you, I'd make my case very strongly before I get there and start working on him."

He frowned. "This ain't right, Carrie Sue, I—"

She cut him off. "No, it isn't right. Now you turn right now and take these hooligans out of here, or you aren't going to like what I tell Daddy when I get home."

Silbee's usual dispassionate reserve seemed strained as he responded. It wasn't in him to allow himself to be bossed around by a wisp of a girl, but his military logic included a clear understanding of when a strategic retreat was called for. He looked over at Jay. "This ain't over, boy."

"Never figured it was," Jay responded with a grin. "Thought you said you weren't going to call me boy anymore."

"I lied."

Silbee dug his spurs into the gelding's flanks and rode off. The cowboys followed. A couple of them shrugged and aimed sheepish glances at Carrie Sue. There wasn't an unattached cowboy in a three-state area who wouldn't give a year's pay for a chance with her. She turned her shoulder to them and tossed her hair. They hadn't made any points with her today.

As they watched Silbee ride off with his cowboys, Paco said sadly, "Señor, I fear we are now on his bad side for sure."

Jay nodded. "I ain't never been nowhere else, but I told you that you shouldn't stand with me."

"A man must do what is right, Señor, no matter the cost."

Jay stood thinking for several minutes as Paco's wife walked up to stand beside her husband. "Your place in town, ain't it pretty small for such a big family?"

"Rosita and I have a bed," Paco said, taking his wife's hand in his, "but there is little space in our one-room *casa* for the children to make a bed on the floor."

"That's the answer then. We can do better than that. We have a bunkhouse that'll sleep you all, and we don't have cowboys anymore to need it. We got some old barn lumber we can use to close off the end so you and Rosita can have a room to yourselves."

Rosita clasped her hands together, and her dark eyes sparkled. *"To ourselves?* Oh my, not since we were first married ..."

Paco smiled. "I think you have your answer, Señor."

"You know we can't pay you," Audrey said.

"It is no matter," Paco replied with a shrug. "You have a garden, do you not? We have much mutton. I have young sheepherders. When you have money, you can perhaps pay something then?"

"Of course. We can raise sheep on shares. When we have money, you'll have money."

"And there is safety in numbers, Señora. We shall eat, we shall work together, and we shall have room for the *niños* to sleep in real beds. It will be a better life than we have ever had."

Four

*C*olonel Johnson stood on the porch as Silbee rode up. "What on earth happened to you?"

The cowboys rode on to the barn. One paused to take Silbee's horse after he stepped down to join the colonel. "It was that sheepherder, sir. I didn't see him slip up behind me."

Johnson looked closely at his foreman's face. The impassive facade still showed the unmistakable marks of battle. "He did that to your face from behind you?"

Silbee didn't want to talk about it, but years of discipline made it impossible for him to ignore a superior's questions. "He tapped my shoulder, and I turned right into it," he said in a subdued voice.

The colonel walked to a large overstuffed chair and dropped into it heavily. "Even at that, a mere boy taking out one of the army's toughest sergeant-majors? Unthinkable."

"Not one of my best days, sir," Silbee said glumly. He moved to the chair next to the old man and eased into it.

"Very well, Sergeant, do you have a report on the patrol for me?" Johnson took out a cigar and used some clippers to trim the end. "Stay seated," he said as Silbee started to rise to his feet.

"Yes sir. I took the troop ... er ... the hands out to finish the job on that herd of sheep."

"I think that if they are sheep they are considered a flock, not a herd. Continue, Sergeant."

"A flock, yes sir. When we arrived back on the scene, we found that the enemy had been reinforced. Mexicans, sir."

Johnson froze in the act of lighting his cigar. "You don't say. How many men?"

"Only one, sir. Also a woman, two young boys, and three young girls."

"Harrumph, that doesn't sound like reinforcements to me." He grimaced as the match burned too close to his fingers, then tossed it into the yard and fired up a fresh one.

"They were helping them regroup, sir; that's what reinforcements do."

"Very well, did you disperse them?"

"That wasn't all of the reinforcements."

"More? Who this time?" He got the end of the cigar glowing and then blew a long blue cloud of smoke.

"Your daughter rode up and stopped us."

"Stopped you?" He glowered. "Since when do you take orders from my daughter?"

"Since she said I would have to go through her to do anything to them. I figured you wouldn't want that, sir."

"No, quite right. Your mission was not a success then?"

"No sir, we had to retreat. Reckon by now the enemy has successfully regrouped. I'm sorry, sir."

"It sounds as if it was out of your hands. Never have female children, Sergeant. They are impossible to control."

The two men were so engrossed in their conversation they hadn't seen her coming. "That's what you get for wanting to control everything around you." Carrie Sue stood at the edge of the porch, a disapproving look on her face.

Her father knew what that look meant. "Sergeant, tell her ... Silbee? How does he disappear like that?"

Carrie Sue walked over and perched on the arm of his chair. He knew very well she was about to try to manipulate him. She didn't disappoint him.

"Daddy, did you really send all those men over there to jump on those poor people?"

"Of course not," he blustered. "I gave no such orders. I merely indicated that I wanted those sheep kept dispersed. I want it done until they give up on keeping the smelly animals. At that point I will offer Mrs. Mendelson a fair price for her land, and everything will come out all right. I want no one hurt."

"If that's true, then the intent of your orders is not being followed." She put her arm around his neck. "Promise me, Daddy dear, that you will rein in Silbee. He's out of control."

"I will, Carrie Sue." He stroked her hair. "You are so very much like your mother."

"You miss her, don't you?"

Sadness settled into his features. "More than you know, dear. More than you know."

They sat around the table in the center of the bunkhouse eating mutton stew and flour tortillas. Rosita hummed as she patted out the tortillas by hand then dropped them on the stovetop to cook. The Gonzales family had never had such room or such a fine wood stove to cook on. They felt wealthy. Jay and Audrey enjoyed the company. It was good to have the young people bringing life to the ranch.

"You were a *vaquero*, a cowboy, yes?" Paco searched Jay's face for answers.

"For many years." Jay knew where this conversation was going, but the little man had put his life on the line for him. He deserved some answers. He waited for him to put his concern into words.

"Señor Jay, I am confused. Cowboys, they have this bad feeling toward the sheep. I have seen it, yet here you are fighting for them."

"They've kinda grown on me, I have to admit. They're funny critters. You know, even rabbits can defend themselves with their hind feet if you grab them, but not sheep. They're totally defenseless. Lady and I are all they have to protect them. That kind of dependence gets to you after awhile."

Five

*I*s the colonel mad because we let that sheepherder get away?"

The three hard cases sitting on the fence weren't working cowboys. They were gun hands, pure and simple. They stayed out of the colonel's sight or made a show of working to keep Johnson from being fully aware that they didn't have any function in the day-to-day operation of the ranch. He didn't know the trio was Silbee's private army, leftovers from the war.

The working hands knew, but they weren't talking, particularly if it meant incurring the wrath of the one speaking now. Hank Peyton was a huge man, mean to the core. All three men had the same cold, calculating approach to life that ruled out emotion and compassion and made them perfect companions for Silbee. Peyton's size made the diminutive Sam Carter, on the fence next to him, seem even smaller than his five feet six inches. Carter made up for his size with quickness, both with a gun and a knife. He had dark features, accentuated by black hair, eyebrows, and mustache.

The third man, Frank Williams, had a guileless look on his round face. Williams was not a heavy thinker, but he obeyed orders without question.

Silbee walked over to them. "I made a mistake. I shouldn't have shot the dog. People love dogs, and everybody is on me about it. I shoulda shot the sheepherder. Nobody likes a sheepherder."

Peyton let out a mirthless laugh. "It's not too late."

"No, it's not. We'll correct that mistake. I made another mistake too. I shouldn't have taken all the working hands along on the raids. I thought that'd make it all go down better with the old man, but they listen to the girl too much. They'd roll over and let her scratch their bellies if she asked."

"We don't need them," Carter said. "It ain't like he's really got any help."

Silbee nodded. "We need to get him off by himself, out away from all those snot-nosed kids and that widow lady. People get nearly as upset over them as they do about a dog."

Williams turned with a look on his face as if he had just awakened. "How about the Mex?" he asked.

"He's a grown man. He can take care of himself."

Sheriff Ron Farnsby rode his big steel-dust stallion up to the headquarters of the Circle J. He was a frequent visitor since Colonel Johnson had single-handedly put him in office. He stepped down, tied off the reins, and holding his hat aloft with his left hand, used the fingers of his right to rake his golden hair into place. He set his hat carefully back into position and then with the tip of his right pinkie smoothed down his eyebrows.

His sights had been firmly locked on Carrie Sue for some time as the key to the eventual ownership of the huge ranch. Farnsby was nothing if not ambitious.

He locked a dazzling smile on his face, one sure to overwhelm any mere female, and knocked on the huge oak doors. The maid, Esmeralda, answered, and Farnsby's polite demeanor disappeared. His tone indicated a disregard for a simple servant.

"The colonel here?"

"*Sí*, Señor, will you follow me, please?"

She led him into the study. "If you will make yourself at home, I will tell him you are here."

"Well, hurry it up, girl, I got things to do."

"Yes, Señor, may I take your hat?"

He relinquished the Stetson with the four-inch brim, pausing in the exchange to fleck a spot of something from the crown. Esmeralda scurried off. Farnsby hooked the thumb of his left hand into the polished black gun belt and ambled around the room.

He wasn't used to giving up his hat; it was generally the first thing a Western man put on in the morning and the last thing to come off at night. He hadn't allowed the maid to take it the first time he had come, and the colonel had immediately asked him if his head was cold. Another of his little games.

He stopped at the table where liquor sat in cut-glass decanters and selected what he knew to be a fine Kentucky Bourbon. He poured himself two fingers of the fiery liquid and helped himself to a cigar from the humidor before he resumed his stroll around the room. It was lavish for these parts, rich cherrywood shelves full of books framing the dark mahogany desk. He thought he would have a house like this one someday. Maybe he would have this one.

The colonel's voice cut into him. "When people drink my liquor or smoke my cigars, it's generally because I have offered it to them."

Farnsby choked on a swallow. "Sorry, Colonel, it's just that you usually offer—"

"That's the operational word, all right, 'offer.' I don't like people taking liberties with anything that's mine."

Farnsby set the glass back on the table.

"Sorry, sir, I just wasn't thinking."

"Well, don't put it back now, you fool. No point in wasting an expensive drink." Johnson knew what he was doing. He was an old hand at using ploys such as this one to establish his authority and put men in their place. He couldn't care less about someone having a drink.

"Have a seat."

Farnsby moved to the chair next to the desk, but the colonel pointed to the chairs straight across the big mahogany monument and said, "No, over there."

More games.

Johnson leaned back in the big leather desk chair, steepled his fingers, and said, "What's this all about? It can't be social because you weren't invited."

Farnsby looked pained. "No sir, it ain't no social call."

"What then?"

Farnsby scooted forward in his chair. "It's shooting up that sheepherder's camp, Colonel. All of Three Forks is talking about it. It don't look right for me to not be looking into it or anything."

"Why would you need to look into it? You know who did it, and I can't believe the town cares one ounce about a bunch of sheep."

Farnsby squirmed as if he couldn't get comfortable in the big chair. "Nobody cares spit about the sheep, you're right there, but it don't sit right with a lot of folks to be harassing a widow lady."

"And when *all* of these people come to you demanding action, and I presume they *are* demanding action, how do you respond?"

Farnsby tried to sit back and look confident but failed to pull it off. "I tell them I'm looking into it, of course."

"And are you looking into it?"

"That's why I'm here."

"Very well, Sheriff, you may go back and tell these concerned citizens that the deed was apparently perpetrated by a band of liquored-up cowboys on their way home to another county. You will say it was unfortunate, but understandable given the way cowboys feel about those nasty creatures."

"Yes sir, I can do that. Reckon I can tell them it's not going to happen again, that I've taken care of it?"

"Not unless you know for a fact that cowboys have given up drinking in the area, or that the sheep have been removed from the valley, one or the other."

"People aren't going to like that."

"They don't have to like it."

The colonel made a dismissive gesture with the hand holding the cigar. "That little hole in the road would dry up and blow away in a week if the Circle J quit doing business there. They know that. They may complain, but nobody is going to do a blessed thing about it."

The colonel got up. "Is there anything else?"

Farnsby scrambled to his feet. "Oh no, sir, sorry to have to bother you with this."

"Not at all. When you have a problem, it's best to come see what the proper way to handle it is."

He showed Farnsby to the study door where Esmeralda handed him his hat and quickly disappeared.

When the colonel turned his back on him, Farnsby stood there awkwardly for a moment, then headed toward the door. He spotted Carrie Sue sitting on the third step of the broad staircase leading to the second floor. The dazzling smile came back. "Why, hello, Miss Carrie Sue."

"Hello, Sheriff."

"When are you going to start calling me Ron, Miss Carrie Sue? I've asked you to a hundred times. As long as we've known each other, it just—"

"Save your breath, Sheriff. I know you'd like to come courting me."

Hat in hand, he leaned on the ornate banister post. He turned up the candlepower of his smile. "I've made no secret of that, Carrie Sue."

"And you think standing by while my father runs roughshod over some poor people who are doing nothing but minding their own business is the way to impress me?"

Farnsby wasn't used to a woman who could hold eye contact with him, and the look he was getting now had steel in it.

He looked puzzled. "But it's *your* father that—"

"I didn't think the law was for sale, not even to my father."

He moved over to sit by her on the steps. "Of course the law's not for sale, but I've always valued the colonel's opinion."

"To the exclusion of any other, I'd say, and I didn't ask you to sit."

He jumped up as if the step had suddenly become hot. "You know that ain't true. I answer to the voters."

"Most of whom work for Daddy or owe their living to his patronage."

"You said it, not me. You of all people oughta know that—"

"Oh, pooh." She cut him off by rising quickly and going up the stairs. He again found himself standing awkwardly in the hallway. Esmeralda appeared again and opened the door for him.

He stalked out without a word.

Six

Danny Cook looked out the window of the jail as Farnsby rode up. "Oh, man," he said aloud as he saw the thundercloud on Farnsby's face. "She did it to him again. I'm getting out of here; ain't nobody in the jail to look after now anyway."

The potbellied deputy grabbed his misshapen hat from the peg on a hasty retreat out the back door.

The door slammed back against the wall. Farnsby stalked into the room. He pulled off the big white Stetson, started to sail it into the corner, then on second thought pulled his bandanna to flick dust off it before hanging it carefully on the peg.

"Danny." He walked heavy-footed into the back. Cook had called it correctly. Farnsby needed somebody he could kick around to get his self-esteem built back up, and his options were limited.

"Where is that fool deputy?"

He frowned at the emptiness of the room. He retrieved his hat and turned to head over to the saloon. The drunks and idiots who hung out over there would do nicely.

Even with the help of the boys, it was difficult to move the flock without Lady. Jay knew he was dependent on the little Border collie, but he never realized how much until she wasn't there. *Ain't that the way of it?* he thought. *Man never realizes what he's got until it's gone.*

The general direction wasn't a problem as Juan, Paco's oldest, led the way with the bell sheep on a rope. Most of the flock followed the sound of the bell, but sheep were notional creatures, and there were constant excursions on all sides. These side trips were all in a day's work for Lady, and she controlled them easily. For Jay, Paco, and the boys, they were exhausting.

It was less work when the animals began to graze. They spread out, but since the grass didn't grow much up in the tree line on the slope, they were fairly restricted to the gentle hills down in the valley. The workers boxed the flock on four sides and settled in.

Paco and the boys watched the flock, corralled an occasional errant lamb, and kept their staffs ready at hand to repel any animal that might try to grab an easy meal. Jay didn't have a staff, but he did have his Winchester, and he didn't watch over the flock as much as he watched over the shepherds.

Sheriff Farnsby pushed open the batwing doors and paused in the doorway to catalog the place, let his eyes get accustomed to the dimness, and make sure everybody saw him so he could make a satisfactory entrance. As he approached the bar he admired himself in the mirror, the best looking glass in town. He turned his head slightly to get a view of his strong profile, lifting his chin as he did so. He wondered how Carrie Sue could fail to be swept away by his charm; he was pretty sure most women could not resist it.

As if to prove the point, two dance-hall girls came to his side, each taking one of his arms, both fawning over him. They were good for his bruised ego.

He ordered drinks for them and himself, tossed his down, then turned to face the room. In this place he was king. There were the usual half-dozen drunks and lowlifes that he expected to find, and one rancher sitting in the corner nursing a beer before he started the long ride back out to his place.

The bartender filled a mug, and Farnsby carried it over to where the good old boys were sitting around a poker table. This was an unexpected honor for them, and they reacted accordingly.

"I've got me a problem, boys," he announced as he pulled a chair around so his back wouldn't be to the front door.

It was unlikely anybody was going to come in gunning for him; he was more interested in being able to talk freely without anyone walking up on him unnoticed.

"My friend Colonel Johnson has a sheepherder running those smelly critters practically on his doorstep, but legally there's not a thing in the world I can do about it." *And I sure can't let Carrie Sue catch me taking a hand in it,* he thought.

If he was ever to have a chance with her, he figured, two things had to happen. That pain-in-the-neck

Mendelson had to be run out of the territory or disposed of, and when it happened, he had to be as pure as the driven snow in his involvement with the task.

These idiots might be just the things to meet both his needs.

He took a long draw of his drink, and those around him followed suit. He pulled out a bandanna to wipe his lips, and several paused in the act of wiping their own mouths with their shirtsleeves. They looked uncertainly at each other, then shrugging, wiped away. Farnsby continued to hold the floor.

"I don't know what kind of man would bring sheep into cattle country, but it's downright criminal when it's a man that used to run cattle himself."

Most of them frowned. What little work they had done was generally as day hands on one of the ranches around the area, and they surely considered themselves cowmen. They all knew they were supposed to be incensed by the presence of the sheep, though it was doubtful that one of them could explain why. Still, the fact that the sheriff disapproved of the animals was more than sufficient reason for them to do the same.

Farnsby called out to the bartender to bring a pitcher of beer. He needed these men to be as pliable as possible before he worked his will on them. He sat ruminating out loud about how no self-respecting cowman could live with the presence of the sheep, going on and on until he had worked his unsuspecting listeners into a state of righteous indignation.

"What we need is some good old-fashioned night riders to go put some fear into that sheepherder."

"Sure 'nough, that's what we need, some night riders," one of the men said. He sat there for a couple of minutes with a blank look on his face before he added, "What's night riders?"

"Night riders are a group of good citizens who finally get enough of this stuff and take matters into their own hands. As a sheriff I don't approve of such activity, of course."

He had to be careful on this part, or he could talk them back out of it. "But there are some times, when in the name of justice, a lawman has to look the other way and let justice take its course."

Another man leaned forward and tried to focus. "And how does somebody go about being a night rider? Are there rules involved? Does it have to actually be done at night?"

"Man," another said, "I hate to ride at night."

Idiots, Farnsby thought. *I may have to get some chalk and draw pictures on the wall.*

He measured his words slowly. "That's where the name came from; it's generally done under the cover of darkness. The riders usually wear masks made out of flour sacks with eyeholes cut in them and carry flaming torches. It makes them look mighty fearsome."

Fearsome! He could tell it was a concept that appealed to them. Nobody had ever taken any of these guys seriously, and as the word sunk in they gave knowing looks to one another.

Farnsby smiled. That hooked them.

He talked for a bit about how groups he had seen before had worked. When he was sure they had the concept he said, "I'll have to step in and restore order afterwards, of course, but I won't make any effort to find out who's involved. After all, these are just good citizens trying to right a wrong."

Farnsby figured that one more pitcher might bring their courage to the desired level, without making them too drunk to actually accomplish the task. He ordered it, then indicated he had to go make his rounds. That meant he would go back and put his feet up on his desk, as nobody had ever seen him actually out rattling doorknobs.

Darkness made the flock easier to handle. Sheep were terrified by shadows, noises, virtually anything, and by nature jammed themselves together in the darkness for protection. Jay and his helpers took turns watching over them without Lady. If she were there, she could sleep near the flock and still be alert to any possible danger. Without her, they had to actually stand guard.

Jay built a fire over to the side and heated some beans and tortillas. Paco and the boys would not come in until called; then they would take turns handling night watch. Jay was just about ready to make that call when an apparition appeared over the crest of the hill. He and the boys heard the riders before they saw them, a chorus of periodic sneezes.

The sheriff should have been more explicit about the need to wash the flour sacks to get the flour dust out of them before cutting eye and mouth holes to convert them to masks.

The group did look the part though. They were as fearsome in appearance as the sheriff had described; their masks ghostly in the flicker of the torches they carried. The yells as they rode down the slope were ghostly as well, muffled by the cloth over their mouths. It worked on the sheep, and they broke ranks to flee headlong up the slope. Paco was in front of them, but he was powerless to stem the tide.

Jay jumped to his feet and levered his rifle. The boys were in the path of the intruders. He broke into a run as the masked men barreled down the hill. He had taken only a few steps when horses and men went down in a heap. A couple of torches sailed through the air like meteors. Juan and his younger brother Sergio closed on the struggling men with their staffs in hand and began to deliver solid blows right and left. A couple of the night riders went down hard.

One struggled to his feet clawing for his pistol when Jay ran out and nailed him alongside the head with the stock of his rifle. It made a sound like a ripe gourd falling off the back of a wagon.

The boys continued to beat the prostrate raiders until all lay still except one who backed away from Jay pleading. "I'm through. I'm through. This night-riding stuff ain't all it's cracked up to be."

Jay closed the distance. "Jasper? Is that you? You ain't smart enough to come up with something like this on your own. Who put you up to it?"

"Farnsby told us if we was good citizens we'd come do this."

"I should have known. So much for upholding the law." He looked around as he tied Jasper's hands behind his back. "Any of these other characters still got any life in them?"

"No, Señor," Juan said. "I am thinking they are taking the *siesta*."

Jay let his rifle hang down loosely in his hand as he addressed Paco's sons. "You boys were mighty brave, but I don't want to see any more of this."

"If something comes for the sheep, we must protect them. It is what shepherds do."

"That's all right if it's an animal or something, but I don't want you taking on no men, even if they are as addled as this bunch, you hear me? Anybody else would've shot you before you got to 'em."

"What made them fall down in such a manner, Señor? The work, it was done for us."

He grinned. "That rope I strung at knee level across the pass might've had something to do with it."

The boys laughed heartily as they realized what he'd done. "You boys go round up their horses while I stomp out these little fires."

The grass was green, and the fires weren't spreading very quickly. He stamped them out, and the boys soon came back with the horses. They loaded the men on the animals, tied their feet in the stirrups, and then fastened the stirrups together under the bellies of the horses. They finished the process by securing the riders' hands underneath the horses' necks.

They left the masks in place as they walked the animals to the top of the ridge, pointed them toward Three Forks, and then swatted them on the rump with their hats. The animals wouldn't stop running until they got to the livery stable.

Seven

The horses whinnied and pranced in the street, impatient to be relieved of their burdens and put in their stalls. The noise made an urgent counterpoint to the incessant coughing of the men breathing the flour dust in the sacks. The strange sounds brought townspeople out into the street.

Yet, as strange as the sounds were, they were nothing compared to the even more bizarre sight that greeted the townsfolk. They came out to find the street full of masked men making strangling noises as they were hugging their horses' necks. The townspeople gave each other incredulous looks, which slowly changed to smiles, then to laughter, and finally to guffaws.

The masked men pleaded to be freed, but it was several minutes before the townspeople could control their laughter enough to attend to them.

Sheriff Farnsby stepped out on the boardwalk and yelled, "What's going on here?"

It was a tactical error, as one of the masked men, hands finally freed, sat up, pointed, and said, "This is all your fault, Sheriff; you got us into this mess."

Any thoughts Farnsby had of these lowlifes doing the dirty work, while allowing him to be the white knight to set things straight, disappeared in the looks the townspeople gave him. They demanded an explanation, and even though Farnsby tried to intervene, the men being freed of their bonds were more than happy to explain. They were all trying to talk at once when Jay Mendelson rode up, tied off his horse, and stepped out into the street.

"You stay out of this, Mendelson," the sheriff blustered. "I'm investigating this situation, and I don't want no private citizen taking things into his own hands."

"That so?" Jay closed the distance between them. "That's not what I'm hearing. I think the townspeople are hearing the same thing, that talking private citizens into taking things into their own hands is exactly what you've been doing. That how you folks heard it?"

The townspeople nodded and made affirmative noises. The lanterns several of them held high made their faces look even more severe.

"You can't believe what this barroom trash says," Farnsby said. "They're common drunks."

By that time most of the men had been freed and took exception to the characterization with a chorus of denials. None of them had the courage to get physical with the big sheriff though.

Jay was a different case entirely. "I don't blame 'em; they're just good old boys that you liquored up and then took advantage of them. I'm not here for them; I'm here for you."

"Me? I'm the law. One word from me, and my deputies will—"

Before the words were even out of his mouth the two men with badges, who had been standing on the porch, turned and went back into the jail. The message was clear.

Farnsby was nervous. He knew what Jay had done to Silbee, and he was under no illusions that he was as tough as the old cavalryman. The last thing he wanted to do was tangle with Jay Mendelson.

"Looks like you're gonna have to get it done without those deputies." Jay's smile was cool, calculating. He was enjoying this.

Farnsby looked at the townspeople. "Are you going to stand there and let him make a mockery of the law?"

The storekeeper, Scott Walton, said, "He's just one man. What kind of sheriff is it that can't enforce the law against one man?"

"That's just it," Jay said. "I don't think he's enforcing the law. I think I'm here to make a citizen's arrest on him for talking these men into being vigilantes."

"You can't do that." Farnsby slowly backed up as Jay advanced. "I'm the duly sworn law here, and you can't ..."

Jay steadily advanced on him. "Oh, I just think I'll citizen arrest you and let the judge sort it out. He may say you're right."

"But ..."

Jay was through talking and hit the bigger man full in the mouth. The blow spun him halfway around, and he ended up dangling on the hitching post like a child's doll. On the outside Farnsby seemed to give way, but he reached down inside himself to find something he didn't know was there.

With a growl he pushed himself off the post to rush Jay. Jay met him coming in with a stiff-armed punch that stopped the bigger man cold, dazed him, and rattled him to the core.

Farnsby rocked back on his heels, but as his weight came forward he recovered enough to throw a huge punch of his own. Jay almost ducked under it but took it on the right temple, counterpunching to Farnsby's exposed belly. The air went out of the sheriff in a whoosh, and he stepped back. Jay followed it in and put a hard right squarely on the chin. Farnsby went into the dirt.

"You aren't much for doing your own fighting, are you?" Jay said.

Farnsby came off the ground with a quickness that took Jay by surprise, lifting him up and driving him to the ground under all of Farnsby's weight. It was Jay's turn to have all the air knocked out of him. His vision blurred, and he struggled to clear his head.

Farnsby held the front of Jay's shirt in one big hand and sitting astride of him began delivering short choppy punches in rapid succession with the other hand. He landed three blows before Jay could respond by turning to his left, throwing his upper body across the sheriff's knee. As he brought his weight back, he locked both hands and brought them up beside Farnsby's head, spilling him off to the side.

Both men scrambled to their feet.

"You got more sand than I thought," Jay said, wiping blood from the corner of his mouth. "I won't underestimate you again."

"You're not so tough," Farnsby said, wading in and throwing punches as he gained confidence.

Jay caught the punches on his forearm, each time delivering a short hard counterpunch. It was a quick four-punch exchange before Farnsby stepped back, realizing he was taking the worst of it.

He took one more step back, then immediately aimed a strong kick at Jay's groin. Jay twisted his body to the side causing the intended blow to narrowly miss its target. He grabbed the boot heel and shoved the sheriff's foot up with his right hand.

Farnsby seemed to hang in the air, then hit hard on his back again.

This time Jay came down hard on the man with a knee in his stomach. Farnsby was helpless as Jay measured him for a huge right square on the button. He connected solidly, and the lights went out in the sheriff's eyes.

Jay got up to look down on the inert figure. He looked up at the deputies who had stepped back out on the porch. They were making no move toward him. In response to his unasked question, one said, "We didn't figure this for a law deal. It looked personal to us."

"It was personal," Jay said. "Very personal."

Eight

J uan and Sergio were at the fire when Jay returned. "What happened, Señor?"

"I had me this little discussion with the sheriff." Jay stepped down, stripped his saddle, and then hobbled the horse so the animal could graze.

"Did you win or lose?" Sergio was wide-eyed.

"Nobody wins a fight. He was out cold when I left though. Paco on night watch?"

"*Sí*, Señor. He has been out but a short time."

Jay got some water from his canteen to dab at the cuts on his face. "You boys did a man's work tonight. A regular David and Goliath."

"Señor?"

He looked from face to face. "You don't know about David and Goliath?"

They shook their heads, and Juan said, "Do they live around here, Señor?"

Jay laughed. "No, they lived over a thousand years ago. It's a good story; maybe I'll tell it to you sometime."

He wiped his neck with the wet bandanna, then looked at their expectant faces. "Maybe I'll tell it to you now."

Jay moved his saddle over by the fire, spread out his blanket, and made himself comfortable. He poured a cup of coffee before he leaned back against the saddle.

"David wasn't much more than a wet-behind-the-ears kid, not much older than you guys, but like you he was a shepherd. God had already decided that someday David would be the king of Israel—that's a place all the way across the world—but he had a lot of learning to do first."

Juan looked astonished. "A shepherd would be king?"

"Sure enough; that's something, isn't it? Well, it seems these people were having a war about this time, and two armies were facing each other across this big valley. This other army—they were called Philistines—had this huge feller named Goliath that stood over nine and a half feet tall."

The two boys sucked in a breath. "Señor Jay, that is taller than a house."

"It sure is, and he was mighty scary looking. This big guy said that instead of the armies fighting, each side should send out one man to fight each other, and whichever man won, the other side would have to give in and be their servants. But everybody was afraid to fight this big guy."

"Except the shepherd, right?" Sergio was a fast study.

"You guessed it. Well, the king said he couldn't risk it to let a little boy go up against this mountain of a man, but

David said he had once bearded a lion to protect the flock and had killed a bear to protect them too."

"What does it mean to beard a lion?" Juan asked.

"It means that David grabbed the lion by his chin whiskers and held tight while he killed him."

"This David was very brave."

"He sure was. Well the king figured he didn't have any choice since everybody else was afraid to face the giant. He tried to give David a sword and some of his own armor, but David said he'd just use his rod and his slingshot."

"Shepherds' weapons," they said in unison.

"Exactly. Well, when he went out to meet this guy, the big fellow just laughed when he saw David carrying a slingshot and a rod. He said, 'Am I a dog that you would come at me with a stave?' A stave is a stick, and he thought—"

"We beat wild dogs with our staffs to run them off from the flock!" Sergio said. His eyes gleamed. They didn't have to have this part of the story explained to them.

"You're right. Anyway the big guy got ready to take David apart, but the shepherd pulled out his slingshot and a smooth stone, whirled it around, and sent it right into Goliath's head. It killed him right then and there."

"I knew he would win," Juan said proudly.

Jay smiled. "He won because God helped him. I thought of him tonight when I looked up and saw my two young Davids charging the Goliaths. You were both very brave."

"You think God helped us?"

"We didn't have time to ask, but yes, I think he might have lent us a hand."

Sergio said, "It is a good thing."

"Yes, it is, but you remember what I said; no more going up against armed riders, all right?"

"How dare you?" Carrie Sue stood in front of Farnsby's desk. She was in full battle mode.

"Now Miss Carrie Sue, I don't need this. That Mendelson guy you're so fond of jumped me right in front of the whole town. Before I knew what was going on he'd waylaid me."

Farnsby held a wet towel up against his head. "As soon as I get situated, I'm gonna go arrest him for assaulting an officer of the law."

She threw back her head and laughed. "You do, and you'll be laughed completely out of the county. The only reason that hasn't already happened is the fact that you at least stood up to him."

"I did more than stand up to him, if it hadn't been for—"

Carrie Sue cut him off with an upraised hand. "Don't push it. You salvaged a little of your pride; don't throw it away by making some lame excuse."

"No excuses here," he said. "Just weren't right, him not showing respect for the law. No matter what happened between us, he's supposed to have respect for the badge."

Carrie Sue looked at him. *He's pitiful,* she thought, *but for me to have any hope of affecting his activity, I have to make him think the door is still open with me.*

"Please tell me you aren't going to be taking any further steps against Jay. He's doing nothing against the law; I don't care what my father says. I'd lose all respect for you if you did."

"You have my word. I just thought I was doing the right thing for your family. You know how I feel about your family, particularly you."

She lowered her eyelashes, leading him on. "I know, but if you do feel anything for me, you'll respect my wishes on this."

"Absolutely."

Nine

The incision is healing nicely," Audrey said. "Lady is gaining strength by the day, but she's not up to running after a bunch of sheep yet. It won't be long."

They lingered over the remains of breakfast, Jay clearly stalling to delay his return to the flock. He nodded. "We sure miss her. Two grown men and two very active youngsters are hard pressed to do half of what she can do by herself."

She smiled. "Isn't that amazing? But she sure doesn't like being tied up."

They could tell Lady knew she was being talked about. She lay by the fire, head resting on her forelegs, her big brown eyes pleading with Jay.

He made a futile gesture with his right hand. "I know, but there's no other way to keep her from getting back on the job."

Audrey smiled softly. "I keep her in the house with me all I can, but she looks positively despondent when I have to put her on a rope in the yard."

"She could chew through that rope in a heartbeat."

"She's far too much of a lady to do that. If we put her on a rope, she knows we want her there, so she doesn't fight it, but it hurts her feelings."

He went over to the little Border collie and hugged her close. "Hang in there, girl; it won't be long now. We miss you as much as you miss us."

Audrey got up and started clearing the table. "I heard about you telling the boys the Bible story. They were repeating it to the girls. I didn't know Goliath was twelve feet tall."

He continued to rub Lady's head. "Just like boys to exaggerate a good story. It'll probably grow every time they tell it."

"You really made them proud to be shepherds." She set the dishes in the tub and reached for the kettle heating on the wood stove.

"They should be proud. They're hard workers and very responsible." Unable to put it off any longer, he picked up his hat and moved to the door.

She paused from pouring the water and turned to him, concern in her eyes. "Please don't let them take chances like that again."

"I told them they weren't to do that anymore." He tugged on his hat and closed the door softly behind him.

"I sure hope they listen," she said quietly to the empty room. It was almost a prayer.

"I thought those clowns from town were going to do our work for us," Peyton said around the stub of a cigar as

Silbee and his henchmen were playing cards in the deserted bunkhouse.

"Gimme three," Peyton mumbled, throwing his discards into the pot.

Carter dealt him three, Silbee stood pat, Williams took one, and Carter took two for himself. Nobody seemed very interested in the game.

Silbee growled. "Those idiots couldn't hit a barn with buckshot if they were on the inside. Just as well though. After that fracas we had, I'm figuring on getting even with Mendelson myself. I'll raise a buck."

Williams called, Carter threw in his hand, and Peyton stared at his cards as if he couldn't quite make out what they were. "You better be careful with him; you heard what he did to the sheriff, didn't you?" He looked at the cards a little longer, then tossed them with a look of disgust.

"Farnsby is a pansy. My Aunt Martha could take him without breaking a sweat." Silbee spread his hand. "Three fours."

Williams tossed his hand. "Don't you ever lose?"

"Not if I can help it."

While the cards were being shuffled, an unspoken comment hung in the air like Peyton's cigar smoke.

Silbee knew it. "So he took me too, but I wasn't ready for him. I will be next time."

"Why would you want to bother?" Williams gestured at a gun leaning against the wall by his bunk. "I still have my old sharpshooter rifle over there. When we were with the regiment, you guys know I done that enemy officer at over five hundred yards. You were with me when we stepped it off."

Carter nodded. "That was a fine shot, all right. Was it

me, I'd a whole lot rather stand off and potshot him than get down in the dirt knuckle to knuckle with him."

Silbee gave a single nod. "The idea appeals to me, all right, but he made me lose face around here, and I need to get it back before we plant his sheepherding bones."

"Nobody thought nothing about that, Rafe. He is half your age, after all."

"That's got nothing to do with it. I'm either the he-bull around here, or I'm not."

"I thought the colonel was the he-bull."

Silbee grunted. "The colonel has always called the shots, but don't kid yourself. He wouldn't be much if I wasn't standing behind him making things happen. It was that way during the war, and nothing has changed."

Carter started dealing another hand. "So what do we do about the sheepherder?"

"*We* don't do anything, not until after I settle with him. Then we take him out, quick and neat," Silbee said.

He glanced over at the rifle with its long metal sighting tube running down the barrel. "Who knows? I may let you have him then."

If the sheriff had a friend in Three Forks, it would have to be his deputy, Danny Cook. Everyone else he either answered to, lorded it over, or in the case of Carrie Sue, groveled in front of.

The deputy was the only one he could really talk to when he was in a mood to do it. If the mood wasn't there, then Cook was relegated to the servant class. Today the sheriff needed to talk.

Farnsby rocked back in the wooden chair, locked his hands behind his head, and seemed to weigh his words before he allowed them out of his mouth.

"I thought I had busted my britches with Carrie Sue for sure after those idiots bungled that raid on the sheepherder."

Cook's responses were always cautious and diplomatic. He never knew when the sheriff's mood, and his own resulting status, might change even in midsentence. "You haven't?" He perched on the edge of his seat, telegraphing his uncertainty.

"She said *if*, Danny. She left the door open. I've got to take advantage of that, have to impress her in some manner. I have to straighten up and fly right."

"How do you propose to do that?"

"Start being the sheriff for real, of course. Show her a sheriff that's his own man, strong and fearless."

Cook tiptoed on through the exchange, "I don't mean to throw cold water on you, but how's the colonel likely to take that?"

"It'll take some real doing, that's a fact. I have to be one thing for her, but pull the wool over her daddy's eyes."

"That sounds like walking a mighty tight rope."

The big sheriff looked as if he had bit into something sour. "Don't I know it? But I have to get it done."

"You think you can win her heart that way? How does Mendelson fit into this deal?"

Farnsby glowered.

Cook cringed; he knew he had gone too far.

Farnsby's feet came down with a thump, and he terminated the conversation. "It'll be really hard to win her over if he's still around. Something is going to have to be done about him, and I sure can't get caught with my hand in the sugar bowl this time."

Silbee stood leaning with both forearms on the third rail of the corral, his right foot resting on the bottom rail.

He appeared to be watching the sunset, but in reality he was deep in thought.

Peyton walked over to him and matched his position. "It's gotta be Mendelson. Nothing else would be eating on you that bad."

They didn't look at each other. "What does? Oh, yeah, I was thinking about what to do to him."

Peyton leered. "Let's ride over there, and we'll hold him while you work him over."

Silbee gave a rueful smile. "You don't understand the situation. He humiliated me in public. My response has to be public, and it can't be with you guys holding him while I do it."

Peyton half-turned toward him. "You think you can take him this time? No offense, boss, but what's changed?"

Silbee gave a single nod. "You're right. I figure if I go against him head to head, it might come out the same way again."

Like Farnsby, Peyton was careful how he handled Silbee. Comments most men would consider having a discussion, Silbee would often consider questioning his authority.

"Call him out with guns," Peyton said.

"I thought about that. I'm not sure I can beat him there either, and if I did, Carrie Sue would make life mighty miserable around here."

"Tough situation."

"There has to be a way; there always is."

They stood in silence watching the sun drop. It seemed the lower it got, the faster it went, a huge orange ball framed in pink and purple clouds.

Peyton took the last drag on his cigarette and tossed it out into the yard. "How about if the boys and I catch him off by himself and soften him up a little. Then when he gets on into town, a little stiffness, and maybe some sore ribs, will make the difference."

Silbee turned to look at the hard man. "You might have something there. That might be just the edge I need."

Silbee wasn't concerned with the concept of fairness, only the outward appearance of it.

Ten

You get what you pay for, Colonel." Silbee stood across the desk from Johnson. "You ain't paying much for a sheriff, and you ain't getting much." By force of habit the position he assumed was very nearly a military parade rest.

Johnson sat toying with a swagger stick he had carried in the war, working it between his thumb and forefinger, holding it head high. "You say he muddied the water for us in town?"

"That'd be putting it mildly. He sent a bunch of saloon dregs to be night riders on the sheepherder. They came back tied to their horses."

The colonel looked puzzled. "The sheepherder's that tough?"

Silbee unconsciously rubbed his jaw. "It don't pay to underestimate him."

The colonel swung his chair to face the big man, "And how did it muddy the water?"

Silbee shrugged. "The town looked at all those guys riding down on a single man and a couple of young boys, and a lot of them are starting to feel sympathy for him."

Johnson slammed the swagger stick down on the desk. It popped like a whip. "I can't have that."

He sat in silence for a few minutes. Silbee waited him out. "Sergeant-major, you have any suggestions about how to repair this damage?"

Occasionally, without thinking, Johnson would revert to the old titles. Silbee didn't object when he did. Being the sergeant-major was the crowning point of his entire life.

"I may have. I'm going to take Mendelson down a notch. I recommend you spend some time in Three Forks, have a drink with some of the folks, talk about how sheep are ruining the range. These people are still cow-country folks; it won't take that much to remind them."

Johnson nodded. "Yes. Yes, that makes sense. How do you plan to take him down?"

"Man to man, sir. He showed me up the other day, and I intend to get even."

"You think that'll resolve things?"

Silbee smiled a crooked smile. "It should help sway public opinion. It won't help the sheep problem, of course. We've got to get rid of him to do that. The widow woman can't stand without him."

The colonel stood there for several moments, assessing the information. He nodded finally and said, "I should be able to buy her out then, set her up nicely in town. That'd look good, and I could use the range."

Silbee chose his words carefully, trying for a tone that wouldn't challenge the colonel's authority.

"If it's that easy, sir, how come you ain't already done that?"

Johnson scowled. "Mind your tongue, Sergeant. I tried that first thing, offered the boy a job, and offered to set her up just that way. They're cussedly stubborn people. Refuse to let go of that scrap of ground. It makes no sense."

"Yes sir."

"I am so very pleased she's doing all right," Carrie Sue said.

She and Jay sat on the edge of the porch watching Lady move around the yard unimpeded. The dog looked to be a little stiff, obviously not back to full speed, yet she seemed to be suffering no discomfort from her activities.

"I think maybe she can go back to the flock with me. She seems to know her limitations and how far to push herself." Jay was intensely relieved. It was more than just needing her help; he had missed her.

"But if anybody even looks like they are going to hurt her again," he added, "so help me—"

Carrie Sue put her fingers to his lips to silence the threat that was coming. "Don't even think that way. With the furor that came from that incident, nobody would dare to hurt her again. Trust me."

His anger boiled to the surface immediately. He fought to get it under control. "You better be right, because if they even try, they ain't gonna like the results."

Carrie Sue was amused by the sudden outburst. "Don't get yourself all worked up over it. Look at her. She's going to be fine."

Lady explored every inch of the yard as if she had never seen it before. Jay guessed she was having to reassure herself that nothing had changed in her absence. She took her new job as night watchman as seriously as she had her herding duties.

"I hope this is all over now." Carrie Sue looked intently at Jay. "I hope we can live in peace."

"You don't believe that, do you?" Jay half-turned to her and took her right hand in his left. "There are still sheep in the valley. Your dad can't let that stand."

She frowned. "I made my position on that subject quite clear."

"I know you did, and I really appreciate it, but it just means they're gonna try to hide what they're doing from you. You watch and see if people don't quit talking and start acting funny when you walk up, changing the subject and such as that. That's a dead giveaway."

Her eyebrows narrowed, an unmistakable sign the remark had hit home. "They're already doing that."

"I thought so."

It was her turn to show a sudden burst of temper. "I hadn't thought anything about it until you said that. I'm sure you're right; they are up to something."

She stomped her foot. "Oh, wait until I get home."

He put a hand on her arm. "No point in getting all worked up. It's just something we have to work through."

"Work through how? How can we finally put it to rest?"

He grinned. "We?"

"I'm in this, like it or not." She hadn't intended to tip her hand, but now that it was out in the open there was no reason to back off.

He grinned. "Oh, I like it all right. As to putting it to rest, I've been thinking on that. I may have an idea, but I'd rather not talk about it just yet. I do know people have to get it in their heads that we're gonna be here, and we aren't going to cave in."

"We need the support of the townspeople," she said.

"The sheriff and his barroom gang helped us there. They came out looking like a pack of fools."

A smile came unbidden to the corners of her mouth. "I'm playing with the sheriff's head a little too. He would really like to court me; did you know that?"

"A man would have to be deaf and dumb to not know that. It ain't like he's making a big secret of it."

"I told him the other day that *if* he had a chance with me, he had to mind his p's and q's."

He scowled. "I don't think I like that."

Carrie Sue turned the smile up to its full dazzling power. "Jealous?"

"Durn tootin'."

"You have nothing to be jealous about. I just wanted him to not be all that sure of himself. If he thinks he still has a chance with me, he's less likely to do something foolish."

"Actually he's just less likely to let you catch him at it. He'll be just like these other people. They haven't changed their plans a particle; they're just working harder to hide them from you."

Eleven

Audrey smiled as Jay came back in the house, Lady at his heels. She said, "Carrie Sue is really sweet."

"She is that," he agreed.

He sat down at the table, and without asking she poured a cup of coffee and set it in front of him.

She got her own cup and sat down across from him. "So what's the story?"

"Story?" He gave her a blank look.

"Do I have a daughter-in-law in my future? What are you two planning?"

Jay flushed a bright red, the color creeping up his neck and into his cheeks. "We're just good friends. I've known her all my life."

"That how she feels?"

"I'm sure it is; we've never talked about that sort of

thing. Good grief, Momma, what are you trying to stir up?"

She was the picture of innocence. "I don't think I'm trying to stir up anything. I just know what I'm seeing, that's all."

She read his face like a book. He could feel her scrutiny, but he couldn't meet her eyes. "I think you're seeing what you want to see. Don't go trying to push me into something."

"I'd never do that. You're just supposed to let your mother know what you're thinking in this sort of thing."

"I just did. Besides, I got no business even thinking of anything more serious with the kind of trouble I've got right now. And with the way her family feels about me."

"Families don't fall in love; men and women do."

"Momma!" The red extended all the way across his face now. He got up hurriedly. "I've got to go relieve the boys at the flock."

He drained the remainder of his coffee and looked down at the dog. "Girl, let's us go see whether you can do this or not."

"You watch her close."

"You don't have to tell me that," he snapped.

Then regretting his tone, he smiled and added, "I'll keep a close eye, and if I think she's doing too much, I'll put her on a rope."

Audrey didn't mind the brusque tone. She knew she had provoked it, made him mad at her, or at the very least a bit perturbed.

She watched him go out and saddle up. She smiled a mother's smile. She also knew what it meant when a young man got that defensive over such a subject so quickly. She already knew that it was going to take him awhile to come to understand.

"There he is." Carter watched the valley through field glasses. He saw Jay ride up. Shortly he saw the two boys walk up over the ridge going back to the ranch house. Jay was alone except for the dog.

"Yeah," Peyton growled. "This is what we've been waiting for." The trio tightened their cinches, stepped into their saddles, and rode down the slope.

Jay watched them coming, picked up his Winchester, and levered a shell into the chamber.

"You bring that rifle off line," Peyton called to him as they rode up. "We're just here to talk, unless you make it a shooting thing."

Jay cradled the rifle in the crook of his arm. "I don't see we got anything to talk about."

Peyton stepped down from his horse. The hair on Lady's neck stood up, and she gave out with a low growl. She knew who these men were.

"You better get hold of that dog." Peyton pointed a finger at Lady as if he were aiming at her to shoot. "We don't have any intention of hurting her again, but if she comes at me, all bets are off."

Jay knelt to put Lady on the rope tethering her to a tree. She looked at him with puzzlement in her eyes. She didn't like the situation. She couldn't protect him tied up on a rope. But she obeyed and lay down, keeping sharp watch on the men.

"That's better." Peyton smiled, but it was a false smile, particularly as it was hidden for the most part by a bushy mustache. There was no warmth in it.

Carter and Williams stepped down. Carter walked

to the fire to heft the coffeepot and see if it contained anything.

"That's not fresh," Jay said.

"It ain't even warm." Carter tossed the pot down. It tipped over, and the coffee began to run out.

That kept Jay's attention a shade too long. He hadn't realized that Peyton had closed the gap on him until Lady hit the end of the leash, snarling. Jay spun, only to catch a rifle butt in the stomach. He folded up.

Carter and Williams jumped to grab his arms and pull him erect.

Jay's head came up slowly, and he fought for breath. "It's gonna be this way, huh? Three on one? I could take you one at a time."

"You might at that," Peyton said. "I ain't interested in seeing whether you can or not." He walked over to Jay.

"Don't mark his face," Carter said. "You know what the boss said."

Peyton dug his fist into Jay's stomach, making his knees buckle, but he was held erect by the two men on each side of him. Peyton dug his fist in again and again, taking care to work on the ribs.

Jay tried not to give them the pleasure, but he grunted more and more as the blows struck. His breath came in short gasps, and his hands trembled. Only the hands of the two men kept him on his feet.

"If I ain't broke a rib, I'm betting I at least cracked one." Peyton grinned.

They let go of him, and Jay crumpled to the ground. The pain muddled his senses, left him incapable of a response.

"That dog is chewing through that rope." Williams

motioned toward Lady as she did everything in her power
to free herself.

"I hope the thing chews through in time, so I can shoot
it." Peyton pulled himself back into the saddle.

"You know what the colonel said about that."

"Wouldn't matter if I had to defend myself." Peyton
grinned.

Carter and Williams mounted, turned, and rode out
with Peyton. It took several minutes for Lady to finish
chewing through the rope. She ran to Jay and began to
lick his face, but he was out cold. She headed for the
Bar-M.

Audrey came out on the porch as Lady ran into the
yard.

"What is it, girl; what's wrong?"

Lady ran to the edge of the clearing, barking, and then
returned to repeat the process. The third time she jumped
up on the porch and began to pull on Audrey's skirt.

"I get it. I'm coming."

Audrey saddled the bay mare to follow the dog. She
rode hard, covering the distance quickly, but Lady stayed
right with her. She gasped as she topped the ridge to see Jay
lying in a heap, and she spurred the horse to get down the
slope quickly. She pulled up, dropped the reins to ground
hitch the horse, and ran to her son.

She saw blood on his shirt and opened it to see the
bruised and bleeding ribs. Just then Paco came riding up on
his mule.

"Señora, what is it? I see you ride out like *el diablo* is
after you. I think I must follow."

She cradled Jay's head in her lap. "Oh, Paco, you're a
godsend. I didn't think about needing help to get him
back. I guess I wasn't thinking about anything but getting

to him. Can you go back to the ranch and get the spring wagon?

She slipped out from under Jay's head and put his saddle behind him to prop him up a little. She removed her petticoat and began to tear it into strips. When Paco came with the water, she bathed Jay's face with it, then began to clean up his ribs. He came around.

Paco mounted, and she called after him, "Please hurry!"

"Who did this to you?" she asked Jay with more than a little anger in her voice.

"Those hard cases that work for the colonel."

"That's what I thought."

As she gently rubbed his ribs with the hot water, he said, "That hot water is kinda soothing."

"You may have some ribs that are cracked or broken." Her voice seemed barely under control.

"Peyton said he figured he had accomplished that. It was kind of like I heard him from down in a well, but he bragged on it."

"He's a beast." She began to wrap his ribs, and he grunted as she pulled the binding tight, winding him like a mummy. She covered an area some six inches above and below the ribs, tying off the ends.

"Can't argue with that," he said through clenched teeth.

"I know this hurts, but it'll help once I get it tight."

"Tug away."

Twelve

*P*aco took Jay into Three Forks in the spring wagon to see the doctor. Audrey mounted back up and took a direct line to go see the colonel. The farther she rode, the madder she got. By the time she galloped into the yard of the big two-story home and stepped down, she carried a full head of steam.

She didn't bother to knock, but barged right in.

The maid tired to intercept her. "Señora, no, you cannot—"

Audrey pushed her flat on her rump and stormed by. She guessed her target would be in his study. She was right.

Sitting at his desk, Blake Johnson looked up as she blew into the room. He put on a gracious smile and got up.

"Audrey, what a pleasant surprise! It's been—"

She interrupted him with a resounding slap that spun him halfway around. "There's nothing pleasant about this, you snake, and I assure you this is no social call."

She drew back to hit him again, but she found herself restrained by the maid and the butler.

Johnson rubbed his cheek tenderly. There was a clear imprint of a hand on his cheek. "There must be some mistake."

Her eyes blazed. "Tell them to turn loose of me, and I'll show you how much of a mistake this is."

He was mildly amused. "No, I don't think I want to do that. What's this all about?"

Carrie Sue swept into the room. "Exactly what I want to know." She turned a glare on the two servants. "Let go of her this instant."

Esmeralda and the butler looked at the colonel. He nodded but moved back behind the safety of the desk.

"What is it, Audrey?" Carrie Sue took both of Audrey's hands in her own. She saw the tears in her eyes. Something was seriously wrong.

"Is it … is it Jay?" Her breath stopped as she suddenly couldn't bear waiting to hear the answer.

"He's still alive, no thanks to his thugs." She aimed the comment at Johnson with her eyes.

"Daddy!" Carrie Sue let go of Audrey's hands and leaned on the desk as if she meant to vault over it after him.

"What is she talking about?" Carrie Sue's words were clipped, measured, hard.

He put his hand in his pocket and tried to look casual, as well as innocent, but failed to pull it off. "I have no idea, believe me."

Carrie Sue's face colored as her anger rose. "I don't believe you. You said you weren't going to do any more to them."

He stuck out his chest and clasped his hands behind his back. "I gave no such orders."

"I'm an army brat, remember? I know what happens when men do things against your orders. If you didn't actually tell them to do it, they had to know you would condone it, or they would have never dared."

He was adamant. "I know nothing about it."

Carrie Sue spun to look at the maid. "Esmeralda, go pack my things in a trunk." It was not a request but a direct order, and it sounded like one.

She looked at Audrey. "I'm presuming it is all right for me to come home with you."

Audrey smiled. "You are most welcome."

Johnson leaned both hands on his desk, his face getting red. It was time he took a stand. "I forbid it."

"Forbid!" The anger Carrie Sue had been trying to control spilled out. She spun on her father, fury written on every line of her face.

"Forbid!" she said even louder. "If you want me to put a handprint on your other cheek even more vivid than the one you already have, you use that horrible word on me one more time."

She glared at him for a couple of moments before finishing her instructions. "Esmeralda, have a couple of men load my trunk into a buggy. My horse and Mrs. Mendelson's horse are to be tied to the back. And I won't go empty-handed. Go to the storeroom and load the buggy with groceries as well, all it will hold."

"Now see here—"

She spun back on her father, and he physically shrank from the look he received. He had faced cannons, regiments of infantry, but never anything like this. He sank heavily into his overstuffed leather desk chair.

Defeated.

He let her leave without a further word.

"Your mother did a mighty fine job on these bindings. I hate to remove them, but I need to get a good look at these ribs." Doc Blanchard was a good friend. White-headed with a craggy face and a bushy white mustache, he always wore a misshapen old suit that testified to the fact that he didn't practice medicine for the money.

He removed the bindings to poke and prod, eliciting grunts from Jay. He listened through his stethoscope and finally pronounced that nothing was broken, but he said he thought a couple of ribs were cracked.

"Everybody seems to agree on that," Jay said.

"What does that mean?"

"Nothing, Doc. Private joke."

Doc snorted. "Well it doesn't look like a very funny joke to me." He rubbed down Jay's chest with liniment that warmed and felt very good.

"I didn't say it was funny."

Doc pulled out a couple of leather strips. "I'm going to put these hard pads in here under the bindings this time. They won't be quite as comfortable, but they'll protect the ribs while they knit. That liniment is going to deaden the pain for a while. It ought to give you a little relief. I expect you could stand some about now."

He put the pads in place and began to wrap Jay's torso tightly with gauze. "How did this happen? If it was just one place I might think a horse kicked you, but this looks deliberate."

"I'd say it was very deliberate, Doc. Two of the colonel's men held me while a third worked me over pretty good. They're dead set on discouraging me. They don't know me; it just makes me more rock-headed stubborn."

"Your daddy was the same way; the fruit doesn't fall very far from the tree."

He stopped wrapping and became thoughtful. "You'd best be careful. There may be something else going on here."

"If I was any more careful, I'd be hiding in the root cellar and not coming out." He laughed, but it immediately turned to a grimace, and he laid a hand tenderly on his side. "There's something about people trying to kill you that tends to make a man cautious."

Doc put his hand on his chin as he considered what he was seeing. "I don't understand why they were so careful to work on your ribs but not touch you anywhere that'd show. They have something in mind. As to killing you, if they had wanted to do that, catching you out there alone was a perfect chance. There's some sort of hidden agenda here."

"I wouldn't put anything past them, Doc. I just got to do whatever I have to do."

"Well, you don't waste any time getting back to the ranch, and you let Paco and the boys take care of the flock for a few days to give those ribs some time to heal. Don't you go hanging around town any."

"I'll go straight home. I promise."

Jay struggled into his shirt, then paid the doctor. "Paying in money? Amazing. You don't want to buy some chickens or pigs, do you? That's how I usually get paid. I've got a pretty good stock I could sell."

"I might at that. We're getting kinda tired of mutton."

Jay leaned on Paco as they walked out to the wagon to go home. Every step jarred through him. A good night's sleep was starting to sound very good. If only he could buy some time to knit now, time to ... to ... he let out a deep sigh of resignation. Rafe Silbee stood by Jay's wagon.

Silbee moved in line to block his path. "We got something to settle," he said.

The doctor was right; there was a hidden agenda, and now he knew what it was. "This isn't right, Rafe," Doc said. "This man is under my care."

"You mind your own business, Doc. You don't want any part in this."

"You think this town is going to let you do something to the only doctor? You're smarter than that. Come to think of it, the way you're going you're probably going to need me yourself."

"Stay out of it, Doc. You can't count on him to make the smart play," Jay said. He turned to Silbee and added, "We need to put this off for a couple of days, Silbee. After your boys got through with me, I need a few days to heal."

"Yellow? Making excuses?"

Jay separated himself from Paco, feeling little chance of walking around this challenge. "You know I'm not. I tore your woodstack down good last time. You let me get on my feet, and I'll do it again."

Silbee had orchestrated this incident nicely. Jay could see that there was quite an audience, but they were on the boardwalk, too far away to hear what they were saying. He saw that Silbee wasn't going to take no for an answer.

If a fight was inevitable, maybe he could even it up some by getting in the first lick. Without another word, Jay hit Silbee hard, right in the teeth. His side screamed at him, but he followed up the punch with two more, driving the former cavalryman back and down. The pain intensified with every blow.

Silbee came off the ground with a rush, driving Jay back into the side of the wagon. Jay's senses swam from the pain even with the pads. Had the doctor not put them on the ribs, he probably would have passed out.

He tried to elbow Silbee, but it was ineffectual. Silbee went to work on his ribs, driving in punch after punch. Jay pulled his arms tight against him, holding his ribs, protecting them. That opened up his head, and Silbee took advantage of it. Silbee drove a huge roundhouse to Jay's head, and he went down hard.

Jay's head spun like a whirlpool, and everything in him told him to get up. He could; he had enough of his senses intact to do it. Yet far in the back of his head a voice said, *There's no dishonor in staying down. You know it's a no-win deal. You can't beat him in the condition you're in, so minimize the damage.*

"What a mama's boy," Silbee crowed, loud enough for the crowd to hear. "Guess it's clear the other day was just a fluke, ain't it? Let's go to the Four Aces. I'm buying."

As the crowd followed Silbee down the street, slapping him on the back, the doctor came out, and he and Paco helped Jay back inside.

The doctor clucked his teeth as he surveyed the damage. "Looks like I've got it to do it all over again."

"He had no chance, Señor Doc."

"I know he didn't, Paco. I guess we know what that hidden agenda was now."

Thirteen

*T*his time Jay went home lying down in the back of the spring wagon. Each bump sent a jolt through his body as if the Devil was prodding him with a pitchfork. He thought maybe he was. Finally the laudanum the doctor had given him kicked in and he surrendered to merciful oblivion.

Paco pulled up in front of the ranch house and got back in the bed of the wagon to help Jay to the tailgate. Jay fought his way back to consciousness to find himself supported by two women. *Two? What's going on?*

"Carrie Sue, what are you doing here?"

"It seems we have company," his mother said. She had a mischievous smile on her face.

"I don't understand."

Carrie Sue looked up at him from her place under his arm. "I've had a break with Daddy. Your mother said I could stay here."

He tried for a grin, but it fell short. "You don't say."

He didn't seem to be able to take it all in. He moved like a man in a dream, swimming through a drug-induced fog.

They helped him to his rope-strung cot and eased him down. Audrey looked down at him, concern bright in her eyes.

Carrie Sue stepped over his leg, her back to him to remove first one boot and then the other. Usually the person having the boot removed would aid in the process by putting a foot on the helper's rump and pushing to help give them leverage. Jay flushed a bright red, testimony that the thought had entered his mind, but he couldn't bring himself to do it.

"You seem to have gotten worse for the trip," Audrey said.

"It was not the trip, Señora," Paco explained. "He was beaten again, by Señor Silbee. He had no chance."

"Silbee," Carrie Sue hissed. "Wait until I get hold of him. He'll rue the day he did this."

"No, you mustn't," Jay held out a hand to her. "Your daddy ain't gonna let you be harmed, and his cowhands will respect that. I don't figure they could hurt you even then, but Silbee is cut from a different bolt of cloth. He's dangerous, and he wouldn't hesitate to hurt a woman—even you."

"He's right, you know," Audrey said. "Best let that lie, unless you can do it in the presence of your father."

"The way I feel about Daddy right now, I'm not sure I could even trust *him* to protect me."

Farnsby walked up to the bar to stand next to Silbee. "I didn't know you had it in you after the last time you two tangled, but you handled him without any problem this time."

Silbee didn't bother to look at him. "I did. And you couldn't. You keep that in mind if you are ever tempted to tangle with me."

The bartender poured Farnsby a full glass of whiskey, and he tossed it down. "Why would I want to do that?"

"You wouldn't, but forewarned is forearmed."

Farnsby got his drink refreshed and began to sip it this time. Trying to talk to Silbee was like trying to dance with a bear; every move had to be measured. "Did I miss something here? I thought we were on the same side. We both answer to the colonel, and we both want that sheepherder out of here mighty bad."

Silbee had been at the bar stewing in his own thoughts for some time. He had reached some conclusions. "When I'm ready for the sheepherder to be gone, he'll be gone. And in case you ain't noticed, the colonel blusters and postures, but I finally figured out that I'm making all the decisions. Besides that, I'm the one taking all the chances. Don't know why it took so long for me to get that into my head."

Silbee tossed down his drink. "It was no different in the war. I led the charges while he waved his sword back in the back, sitting on his big white horse. Then after it was all over, he got all the medals and the glory. All I got was bullet holes in me—not once, but twice. I'm thinking it might be time for me to start getting what's coming to me. But I don't know why I'm telling this to you."

He glanced at Farnsby, not really acknowledging him. "I reckon I'm not. I reckon I'm just admitting it out loud."

"That's dangerous talk, Silbee."

Silbee narrowed his eyes and turned toward the sheriff. The menace was clear. "Dangerous for who, Farnsby? You repeat it and I'll call you a liar, not to mention killing you for it. You better see how the battle lines are laid out. You line up with the losing side, and we won't be taking prisoners."

Silbee held the glaring eye contact until Farnsby looked down. They both got quiet. Farnsby recognized the truth of what he was hearing. Everyone knew Silbee was really the one who called the shots at the Circle J. He didn't want to be on the losing side.

"Are you saying you plan to take over?" Farnsby asked cautiously.

One side of Silbee's mouth went up. It fell short of becoming a smile. "If something happened to the colonel, somebody would have to."

"The Circle J would go to Carrie Sue."

Silbee wanted to see Farnsby's face as he broke the news to him. He half-turned to again look him in the face, leaning on his elbow on the bar. "Carrie Sue moved out. She lives with that sheepherder now."

"*What?*" All of the color went out of Farnsby's face. She had been playing him for a fool. The whole town would know it.

Silbee smirked. "That's right; you had your loop out for her, didn't you?"

Silbee laughed in his face. "You idiot, she's never given you the time of day. She's played you for a fool from the first time she laid eyes on you. Besides, it ain't gonna take much for me to get the old man to cut her right out of his will. Something happens to him, the Circle J is going to be all mine. And trust me, something *will* happen to him."

The dirt I've eat for her, thought Farnsby. *This ain't right. She's gonna pay for this.*

And that sheepherder is a dead man.

Colonel Johnson bought drinks, he had lunch with leading citizens, he acted like a politician standing for election. Everywhere he went he told anybody who would listen that cattle and sheep simply cannot graze the same land.

A lot of people listened.

He found Farnsby in the sheriff's office. "Sheriff, I'm not happy with the way you've been doing your job."

Farnsby thought he wasn't happy with the way Johnson was doing his job either. Maybe it really was Silbee he had to keep happy if he was going to survive this mess.

It was obvious the colonel was just a figurehead, and when they got through with him ... well, Farnsby didn't want to be standing there holding an empty sack. But he had better play his cards close to his vest. Until Silbee made his play, Johnson could still hurt him.

"What's the problem, Colonel?" Farnsby rocked back on the rear legs in his chair; he didn't bother to bring the front feet to the floor.

Johnson looked at the man. There was a change in Farnsby's tone, in his manner. He couldn't put his finger on it, but he was different. "I've been working all day to repair the damage you did with those night riders of yours."

"I admit that idea didn't work out too well, but I was trying to get rid of that sheepherder for you."

Johnson stepped closer to poke him in the chest with a finger. "The problem is, you were doing your own thinking, and you aren't any good at it. In the future you wait for instructions. I'll let you know what to do and when."

Farnsby's eyes blazed. It didn't escape Johnson's notice. In the past the man would have said, "Yes sir," and done some serious bootlicking. Now Johnson saw him sitting there like he'd just eaten a bad steak, and he seemed to be framing a reply. The sheriff obviously *was* thinking for himself. Johnson couldn't have that.

Johnson raised his voice. "I didn't hear your answer."

Farnsby's demeanor suddenly changed. "Oh, sure, Colonel, I'll watch it."

The lack of enthusiasm in his reply made it clear. Farnsby wasn't afraid of him anymore.

Why? What was going on?

Fourteen

*J*ay looked at her with wonder in his eyes. "I can't believe you're here."

Carrie Sue smiled. "I had to leave. Where else would I go but to you?"

"To me?" Jay couldn't believe what he heard.

Audrey peeled potatoes for the stew, not as if it were a chore, but as if she enjoyed doing it. "He thinks you two are just good friends, dear."

"Just good friends?" Her tone got more severe as she turned to him. "When I came and stood beside you facing guns? Is that something that 'just a friend' would do?"

"Are you saying I'm more than that to you?"

"Jay Mendelson! Why would you ask a girl a question like that? It's not up to me to declare myself to you. You're putting the cart before the horse."

There was no way she was going to let him put the entire burden for building a relationship on her. If he wanted to be with her, he was going to have to speak up.

Carrie Sue got up and busied herself helping prepare the meal. Jay lay there in shock. He didn't understand what he had done to deserve the tongue-lashing he had just received.

"Don't be too hard on him, dear," Audrey said quietly.

She glanced over at Jay to make sure she was not being overheard. "Men are not very good at expressing feelings even on their best days. Add to that the fact that he is just now discovering what you and I have known for many months, and you've just got him addled worse than a cat that has run headfirst into the side of the barn. Give him a little time for the notion to sink in."

"Oh, I know that, Audrey." She had a small smile on her face. "But I had to do something to start him thinking about it, didn't I?"

"You certainly did, and nicely done, I might add."

Jay looked at the women across the room, giggling and whispering. He called Paco over. "Paco, did you see what just happened?"

"*Sí,* Señor." Paco sat by the edge of the bed.

"You know what that was all about?"

"*Sí,* Señor."

"You want to let me in on it?"

"Señor Jay, the woman, she owns the emotions, the feelings. The poor male, he lives on the edge, and he tries to understand. My Rosita, she feels deeply, she wants things I cannot give, but I try to give. I love her, and I want her to be happy. Sometimes I do not understand, but always I try."

"I don't get it."

"The señorita has feelings for you that you do not yet share, or maybe you have these feelings but have not sorted them out yet. It is not her place to court you; you are the *hombre,* the man, and it is you that must do the courting."

Jay appeared more confused than ever. "When did I start courting her? I thought we were just good friends."

"She may be your good friend, but you are more to her. It is now your move, Señor Jay. If you have such feelings, you must water them and make them grow. Tell her what is written on your heart. If you do not feel this way about her, you must tell her. Do not allow her to cherish feelings for you if you cannot return them; it is cruel, Señor."

"You are a wise man, Paco."

"Rosita and I have lived long together, produced many fine babies. I love her, and I want her to be happy."

Jay shook his head, somewhat sadly. "I don't know how I feel. I think the world of Carrie Sue, but love? Ain't sure I even know what that is."

"Many men think love is the feeling in their loins when they yearn for a woman. This is not love, but lust. Passion and desire are good for young lovers, Señor Jay, but passion and desire is a torch that must often be kindled anew."

He smiled and put his hand on Jay's shoulder. "But love, my friend, love is when you cannot think of being without her. It is seeing a sunset, and your only thought is wishing she were there to see it with you. It is when you have pain, and only she can ease it, or you have joy, and only she can share it. Love is two people who together make a whole person, and apart they are lonely and miss what is not there. Yes, I know what love is."

"I reckon you do. A lot of that rings true; it really does. You've loaded me down with a lot to think about. I didn't know you were a philosopher."

Paco shrugged. "What is a philosopher but a man who looks closely at his feelings and speaks them aloud?"

Jay laughed. "You are sure enough a surprise to me."

"I think about what I will say, Señor, before I allow my mouth to open and the words escape. Once they are out they cannot be called back. I know taking this extra time causes many to think I am slow-witted, but I would rather be sure before I speak."

He leaned over to take Jay into his confidence. "Besides, my friend, it is often useful to have people underestimate you, is it not?"

Jay nodded. He'd eat a toad before he'd admit that he had been one of those who did just that.

It wouldn't happen again.

"Sergeant-major, I hear you had a run-in with the sheepherder in town." The colonel's tone bordered on direct accusation.

Silbee sat down in front of the desk. "I been meaning to say something about that. The war's been over for some time. Isn't it time we dropped that military stuff? I ain't been a sergeant-major for years."

Johnson made a desultory wave with his hand. "Yes, you're right of course. Habits are hard to break. There are times that I miss the discipline and organization of the military. It has been hard to adjust to civilian life. So many things here seem beyond my control. I presume you don't want to call me 'colonel' anymore?"

Silbee gave a similar desultory wave of the hand. "I don't care. I will if you want me to. I'd think as long as we've been together that we could be on a first-name basis by now. I'd rather be called Rafe."

Johnson's eyebrows rose. "You want to call me Blake? That seems awkward, very informal."

Silbee frowned. "You don't think I'm good enough to be on a first-name basis with you?"

Johnson looked embarrassed. "It isn't that. You know what I mean. It's just a big change. I suppose I'll get used to it."

Silbee got up. "It doesn't matter either way; don't strain yourself." His tone was sarcastic.

He turned and left the room. Johnson realized that Silbee never did answer the question. Like Farnsby, the man had a decidedly different attitude. He felt his control of these men slipping.

Something is going on, and whatever it is, I don't like it.

Hank Peyton sat in the back of the saloon nursing a beer. He was killing time waiting for the blacksmith to shoe his horse. Farnsby collected a mug of his own, walked over and sat down, unasked.

"I feel like the odd man out," Farnsby said.

"What's that supposed to mean?" Peyton said it as if he couldn't care less what the answer was. He considered the sheriff a fool, and he did not suffer fools well.

Farnsby stared into the depths of his mug. "I don't know what happened. A few weeks ago I was popular with the townspeople, slowly winning Carrie Sue over, in good with the colonel, had everything going my way. Now I find out she was just playing me for a fool, and I've lost face in Three Forks."

"What makes you think I want to hear about all your problems?" Peyton snarled. "If you figure we're friends, you're barking up the wrong tree."

Farnsby seemed not to hear him. "And now I find out Silbee is likely to cut the colonel off at the knees."

Peyton's eyes came up, hard and unflinching. He knew it was the alcohol talking. He couldn't care less about Farnsby's whining, but he did care about any mention of Silbee's plans. "You better watch your mouth about that."

His hand went down to the forty-five lying easy in his holster. *Maybe I ought to plug this leak right now.*

"Don't worry, I know better than to say anything to anybody." Peyton's eyes continued to bore into him, making him flustered. "Silbee made it clear I had to choose sides, and if I said anything that got back to the colonel I was a dead man."

"You saying you've chosen sides?" His fingers continued to toy with the handle of the pistol.

"I'm no fool. The colonel's name's on everything, but I know Silbee has been running things for years. Everybody knows it. I ain't figuring on getting crossways with Silbee."

Peyton brought his hand back up on the table. "You best keep it that way."

Farnsby was relieved; he knew where Peyton's hand had gone and why. The same fear that had caused sweat to bead on his forehead had gone a long way toward counteracting the effects of the drink. He wasn't kidding himself about how dangerous these men were.

He gave a weak smile. "I don't see as how I've got much choice no-how. The way things are shaping up, I figure my only play is to string along with Silbee."

Maybe he could let Silbee eliminate Mendelson and the colonel, then use the law to get Silbee. He couldn't do it by himself, of course. But if Mendelson was out of the way, and he was the instrument to avenge Carrie Sue's father and get the Circle J back for her, he'd be sitting in the catbird seat then.

The hard eyes were on him again. If Peyton could read minds, Farnsby knew that he would be a dead man. He held up his mug. "Here's to throwing in with the winning cause."

Peyton didn't drink to the toast, but he seemed satisfied with Farnsby's sincerity ... for the moment.

Fifteen

*T*wo wagons slowly rolled toward the town of Three Forks, the lead wagon driven by Amos Taylor. He wore the white clerical collar and black suit that marked him as a man of the cloth. He stood six feet two inches tall with dark brown hair that matched the thick fringe under his nose.

Amos hadn't always been a circuit-riding preacher. Not so long ago, he had been a rogue and a scoundrel, preying on the unsuspecting, robbing and tricking people out of their money. But that was before God had taken him in hand.

The second wagon was driven by Amos's wife, Judy. Judy was every inch the lady, with long chestnut hair and soft brown eyes. She had had a lot to do with Amos finding religion, but not nearly as much as Joseph

Washington, the old black man riding beside her. He was the preacher's blind sidekick and friend who functioned as his part-time song leader and his full-time conscience. His dark ebony skin made his white hair, beard, and eyebrows stand out as if they were lit up from within.

When Amos had hit town posing as a preacher to cover his nefarious activities, Joseph had seen through him and had been struck by a firm conviction that the Lord was using Amos whether he knew it or not. Joseph had not let up on Amos until he found himself a preacher for real.

The trio was now taking a tent revival on the road. They started by going back to all the places where Amos had robbed and cheated in order for him to apologize and try to set things right. This had proven to be a very dangerous pursuit.

Amos had already been berated, beset, and physically beaten, but God had protected him from being killed. Amos had accepted the rough treatment as his due for his former lifestyle, but more than once he had been narrowly saved from active involvement with a noose.

The three were unaware of it, but they were now making their way toward a town that offered more than its share of additional trouble. It would have made no difference if they had known, however, as Amos went where he felt God led him to go, and for several days he had felt that the Lord had something for him to do in the direction he now headed.

"I don't know what to do. I can't think of anything I haven't tried."

Carrie Sue had tears in her eyes as she unburdened herself on Audrey, sitting in her kitchen. "I made it clear why I was here, didn't I? I did everything but declare myself to him, but it isn't right for me to do that, not right at all."

Audrey put her hand on the back of Carrie Sue's head. "Don't worry, dear, you're doing the right thing. If he doesn't want to be with you, you don't want to try and force him into it. That sort of thing never lasts."

Carrie Sue blew her nose and composed herself. "I suppose I'd rather have him as a friend than not have him in my life at all."

"That's very sweet, but in the long term it wouldn't work. If you two didn't get together and someday he ended up with another, even if you didn't want to distance yourself, his new wife certainly would cause trouble when she discovered how you used to think about him. It's only natural."

"New wife?" Carrie Sue looked horrified. "I don't want to talk about him marrying anybody else."

"Of course you don't; that was silly of me." Audrey sat down opposite her. "I was only trying to make a point. Of course he'll come around. I know my son."

Carrie Sue's eyes moistened. "I'm not so sure. It's just hard to wait, and he doesn't seem to feel any pressure to say how he feels."

"It's different for men, dear." Audrey put a hand on the younger woman's arm. "They don't think the same way we do. He worries about the problems we're facing, things that need to be done at the ranch, the bills, all sort of practical things. Somewhere down the line he may get around to trying to figure out something of an emotional nature, but, unfortunately, even when he does he may not be able to put it into words. They do that, you know."

"Was your husband that way?"

Audrey laughed. "Very much so. We lived our whole lives together, and I can count on one hand the number of times he put his love into words. But I knew he loved me. He said it with his eyes, with his touch, with the little things he did for me. I knew it, and I knew him. It was enough."

"You didn't miss hearing the words?"

"Of course I did, dear. I would have loved to have more romance in my life, but if it meant I had to have someone other than him, I'd rather have him."

Carrie Sue nodded slowly. "I think I understand that."

"I hope so, because in order to understand Jay, you have to understand his father. They really are just alike."

"I'm so glad we talked. I think this helps. It's still hard, but it helps."

Esmeralda came into the dining room to find the colonel picking at his food. She walked over to stand by his shoulder. "Señor Johnson, you must eat. Every meal I come in, and it is the same. You push the food around on your plate, you play with it, but it is still there."

"It isn't the food, Esmeralda. I simply do not seem to have an appetite." He pushed the plate away. Life just wasn't the same these days.

She picked up the plate. "Señor, you must go to her. The house is empty without her."

The colonel stiffened. "She made her bed; she has to lie in it."

"She would say she was pushed from the house, Señor."

"*Pushed?* Don't talk foolishness, Esmeralda. She's taking sides with this sheepherder against her own flesh and blood. Silbee told me I should cut her from my will, and hanged if I don't think I ought to do it."

He pulled out a cigar and bit off the end. He fished in his pocket without success for a match.

"But you love her, Señor." Esmeralda's face was a mask of concern. She had been very close to Carrie Sue, more like a sister than a maid. She stepped to the sideboard, set down the plate, and retrieved a match to light the cigar for him.

"Of course I love her; that makes it all the harder. But if she loved me she couldn't have, couldn't have …"

Esmeralda's face softened. "Couldn't have what, Señor? Stood up to you? You keep saying she is just like her mother, but what I see is a mirror image of her father. If you believed in something strongly, would you not stand up for it? If you felt strongly about someone, and everyone seemed set on their destruction, would you not run to them? Ask yourself what you would do, Señor, then expect nothing different from her."

"You forget your place."

He blew a stream of smoke, then watched it until it disappeared.

"Yes, it is true, but I love her too. I speak out of love, and I hope you do not hate me for what I have to say."

"I don't hate you. I just don't want to hear it. This is hard enough for me to bear without you droning on about it."

He looked at the girl, recognition dawning on him. "You don't have to be here either, do you? You could have gone with her and been welcome. Why didn't you?"

She shrugged. "I told her I would go with her, but she said no. She said you would be alone if I went."

"Alone? I have a ranch full of cowboys."

"Ranch hands you never see unless you ride out on the range, and a butler who only comes when summoned and then is nothing but correct and proper. You would be alone."

"Is that what she said?"

"*Sí*, Señor." She picked up the plate and turned to leave, but she stopped at the door when she heard Johnson speak.

"I'm alone now, Esmeralda, even with you here. I miss her."

"That is what I have been saying, Señor. You must go to her."

His head came up, full of pride. "And tell her I was wrong? She's the one that's wrong."

"Do you feel that way so strongly that you are willing to cut her out of your life like the core of an apple? That is what it means to take her from your will."

"I know what it means," he snapped. "If she's dead set on that sheepherder, you think I want him getting his hands on the Circle J and spreading his sheep filth over the whole range? I'd die first."

"Señor—"

"I don't intend to discuss this with you."

He turned on his heel and stomped out of the room. She heard his study door close and immediately heard the whisky decanter clink its silver note as he poured himself a large portion.

As in nights past, she knew she would continue to hear that sound until the wee hours of the morning.

Jay took his turn watching over the herd as Paco and the boys went back to eat and take a *siesta*. It wasn't a hard task with Lady back on the job. She was so happy to be at work that she appeared to be grinning. She ran around the meadow with no apparent indication of how close she had come to dying.

"I'd say she's happy to be back." Carrie Sue's voice startled Jay from his reverie.

He laughed. "Happy doesn't even come close to getting it said."

He started to get up, but she put a hand on his shoulder to stop him, and then sat down beside him.

He smiled. "And it doesn't come close to how glad I am to see her back to normal," he added.

She lay back, closed her eyes, and drank in the air fragrant with the heavy pitch smell of the salt cedars, the lighter scent of the grass underneath her head. She opened her eyes to see an armada of giant cloudy sailing ships crossing an ocean of sky so blue that it defied description.

She smiled. "It's so beautiful. It's right there in front of me all the time, has been all my life. Wonder why I don't stop and realize it more often?"

He lay back alongside her and propped himself up on his elbow. He didn't look at the clouds, but rather at her. "We all do that. We take things for granted, don't see what's right under our noses."

"Are we both talking about the same thing?"

"Not if you're talking about clouds."

She became coquettish. "Why Jay Lyle Mendelson, whatever could you be talking about?"

"Don't bat those eyelashes at me. You know durn well what I'm talking about. Look, Paco talked to me like I was a black sheep in the flock. He made me understand that if you and me was to start courting, that it was my job to do it, and not yours. But that don't mean I'm gonna do it all; you gotta meet me halfway."

Her eyes looked as if they were liquid pools. "Halfway is good, but halfway to where?"

His face clouded up. "Don't start pushing me. I just now figured out we might be more than 'just good friends.'"

She knew she had to be careful. "I'm not pushing, Jay. Just talk to me. I don't care how long it takes, not if I know what you're thinking. It's uncertainty that I can't live with."

"That ain't easy."

She touched him on the arm with a gentle finger, needing the contact. "I know it isn't. I know sharing what you are feeling doesn't come natural to you. It didn't come easy to your father either; Audrey told me. If you can't share with me, then we may not be meant to be together. If you can, then we'll be closer to each other than we are to anyone else on earth."

"I honestly don't know if I can," he said. Her eyes had a magnetic pull, drawing him in, conveying a sincerity he wasn't sure he could match. He was a greenhorn at this courting business, a newcomer in a game he was sure she had been born knowing how to play.

"We have to start small," she said. "You don't have to tell me you love me, or tell me what's in your heart. Just share something with me. It can be small, not even something important, the sharing is enough. If we just start sharing what we think, we can build on it slowly until we can share what we feel or dream. Then we'll be there."

"I'll try."

"I'll even start it." She sat up, crossed her legs, and clasped her hands together. "Nothing scary like home or kids or such."

She paused to let his curiosity build. "I want a porch."

"You want what?" He sat up as well. This wasn't the sort of exchange he had expected.

"A porch," she repeated. "I've always wanted a big porch that goes all around a house, shading the sun, a porch for sitting and soaking up nature like a big old sponge."

Jay laughed. There was another pause while he gathered his thoughts to respond. "For me it'd be a barn. Not a little thing like we've got now, where we can barely turn around without bumping an elbow, but big enough for stock and tack, and a loft for hay. Doors on either end so the breeze could blow through in the summer."

"That wasn't so hard, was it?"

"Not really."

She took it up a notch. "You see yourself always herding sheep?"

"No. If I could find a way, I'd love to get back to ranching the way we used to do it. We're just getting by the only way we could see to do it."

"Maybe there is a way. We'll have to think on that."

"Together?"

"I'd like that."

Sixteen

Williams sighted down the tube on his sharpshooter's rifle and centered it on Jay's chest. He snuggled his chin against the stock. One slow pull and it would be all over. "I've got a bead dead center on that sheepherder's chest, Rafe. You want me to pull the trigger?"

Silbee looked down into the valley below. Just one word and his problems with the sheepherder would be history.

Williams tightened the pressure on the trigger, awaiting the command. Everything in Silbee told him to say yes ... but he had one small problem. "Not with Carrie Sue there."

Williams eased off on the trigger, looking disappointed. He just couldn't keep up with Silbee's changing plans. "I thought you planned to get rid of her too?"

"Not if it isn't necessary. Killing a woman can stir things up awful bad. No telling how things might work out if that happened. I might have to eliminate her if I can't talk that old fool into cutting her out of his will, but for starters I just need to be rid of that sheepherder. One thing at a time."

"How about if I go down there and tell her that her pa sent for her?" said Carter. "It could get her away from there."

"No, that wouldn't work. It'd be like pointing a big red arrow right at us when they found the sheepherder's body."

Peyton smirked. "You think people ain't gonna know who done it when he comes up dead?"

"What they know, and what they can prove ain't the same thing. Besides, I'm thinking I might be able to pin it on that idiot sheriff."

"That's good thinking."

Silbee mounted. "Well, we don't have to be in a hurry. All it takes is patience."

Williams slid the big gun back into his saddle scabbard, and the trio of gun hands followed Silbee back to the Circle J.

"There'll be another day."

Audrey glared at him as if she could shoot icicles with her eyes. "Colonel Johnson, you are not welcome on the Bar-M."

He made no effort to dismount. "I understand that, Mrs. Mendelson. I came to apologize."

That caught her off guard. "Apologize?"

"Since our last meeting I have become aware of some of the difficulties that you have been experiencing. I do not apologize for wanting those smelly creatures of yours off the range, nor even for sending men to scatter them and discourage you."

"That doesn't sound like any apology I ever heard." Audrey was still aloof, unbending.

He pulled himself even straighter in the saddle. Apologizing was not a natural act for him, and it was taking a lot out of him to do it.

He continued. "I suppose not, but what I came to say is, I did not order nor condone the violence that came to be associated with this action. I did not approve of shooting the dog, and I certainly did not approve of the violence directed at your son. I have expressed this disapproval in no uncertain terms to the appropriate parties."

"So it will stop now?"

His shoulders sagged. "A month, even a week ago, I would have said yes in the absolute certainty that my orders would be carried out. Now ..."

His head drooped. This did not look like the proud military man she had known for so many years.

"I don't understand," she said.

He fought to regain his military bearing, lifting his chin and straightening his shoulders. "Nor do I, madam. My iron grip on this valley is slipping, and I do not know why it is doing so, or what I can do about it. I have always depended explicitly on the men who served me in the war, and now they don't seem to extend me the same courtesy and respect. If we were still in wartime, I would suspect a mutiny. I don't know what I expect now, but the long and short of it is," he sighed, "I cannot guarantee that my instructions will be followed. I will do my best to ensure they are, however; you can rest assured of that."

Audrey looked hard at Johnson for several minutes. She had no reason to trust him, but somehow she sensed that she could.

"Would you like a cup of coffee?"

"I would indeed. It is very lonely over at my house." He stepped down to follow her inside. He looked around as he entered. The house was quite small compared to his mansion, but it was neat and comfortable.

She saw the unspoken question in his eyes. "Carrie Sue is not here. She went to be with Jay up at the flock."

He nodded. "She hates me now."

Audrey placed two settings of her good china on the table and poured his cup to the rim. "Don't be silly. She loves you very much."

"She couldn't still love me or she wouldn't ..."

Audrey sat down across from him and filled her own cup. "She loves my son too. You made her choose, and you made her lose respect for you at the same time. It is quite possible to love someone and not like them. She still loves you, but she doesn't like you very much right now."

He appeared to ponder that statement a moment, and then he nodded. "I accept your evaluation of the situation. I shall have to consider how I can make her like me again."

Audrey took a sip from her cup, appraising him over the rim. "That's a worthwhile goal."

"I don't think I can do it at the expense of allowing sheep on the range. However, right is right, so let me get to the business that brought me over here. I understand that more than fifty of your stock have been killed in these foolish raids. Unnecessary. I have made inquiries into the market price of the animals."

He passed her a bank draft. "I believe you will find that this is adequate compensation for what you have lost. Here is a second bank draft adequate to purchase the entire remaining herd."

"Flock. Cattle are a herd; sheep are a flock."

"I know that," he said, his temper barely under control. "Do we have a deal?"

Audrey picked up one of the drafts. "I will accept your compensation for the animals that were destroyed, because I believe that orders or no, the men thought they were doing what you wanted them to do."

She pushed the other draft back toward him. "However, the flock itself is not for sale. We could not stock it with cattle on that amount of money. Raising sheep is the only means we have of retaining the ranch with what we have available to us."

"I understand that." He pushed the draft back toward her, overlaying it with another piece of paper from his inside jacket pocket.

"Here is a third draft for what I believe is a very generous offer for the purchase of the Bar-M. The three drafts would keep you in fine style the remainder of your life."

She let the papers lie untouched. "My husband worked his whole life to establish the Bar-M, and he wanted to pass it down to Jay. I have no intention of allowing his dreams to fail."

She stood, and he did so as well. She pushed the other two drafts back toward him.

"I thank you for the apology, and for reimbursing us for the sheep. However, I'm still planning to keep this ranch in spite of anything you might do to us."

"I have no plans to *do* anything to you, but I can't

speak for others." He shook his head slowly. "I fear you are being very foolish."

"I am being practical, Colonel Johnson, following the only course I seem to have that allows me to keep from losing the Bar-M."

He straightened his backbone to his usual military bearing. "Very well, Mrs. Mendelson. I shall endeavor to find another way, one that I hope might forestall any further violence."

"I'm pleased to hear you talk like that, Colonel, and I'm sure Carrie Sue will be pleased to hear it as well."

Seventeen

*H*e apologized?" Jay couldn't believe it.

Carrie Sue just smiled. Jay sat at the table, the ever-present cup of coffee in his hand, as the two women prepared something to eat.

Audrey nodded. "Not only that, but he paid for the sheep that were killed."

"Imagine that," Carrie Sue said. "Perhaps Daddy is coming around. He can be so pig-headed."

"And he offered a nice figure to buy the ranch, as well as the remaining stock."

Jay frowned. "You should have taken it. With that much money you could live the rest of your life in town."

"That's what he said too."

Audrey held a pot lid in her right hand as she stirred the contents. "I told him the Bar-M is not for sale. We said we were going to do whatever we had to do to hang onto it. Nothing has changed that I can see." She replaced the lid and turned her attention to another pot.

"Oh no, nothing but a bunch of people trying to kill us."

Something in his tone caused her to turn, surprise on her face, still holding the lid of the second pot. "Are you ready to give up?"

Jay shook his head. "You know better than that. I'm just thinking of what's best for you."

Audrey turned back to the stove. "What's best for me is to hang onto the ranch my husband and my son have fought to keep."

The last thing she needed was for her strong son to lose faith that they could win. She thought he was just worried for her. "I'm going to take Paco with me and go to Prospect," she said, referring to the largest town in the area.

"You gonna buy some more sheep? Don't you want me to do that?" The look on Jay's face made it clear he didn't consider buying stock to be woman's work.

"No, I think I want to do it myself. Please have Paco put the high sides on the wagon, and then ask if he will go over to Mr. Lawrence's house to see if we might borrow his high side wagon for a day or two as well."

"Gonna freight them in, huh? That's good thinking. Much faster than trying to drive the silly things, and you won't run the meat off of them either."

He stood up, drained his cup, and prepared to do as she asked.

"The meal is almost ready; it can wait."

"We probably have time to get those sides on the wagon before you call us."

He put his hat on and walked through the door. His

mother was a much stronger-willed person than he had realized, or maybe it was the situation.

She smiled at his back and then turned to Carrie Sue. "Would you like to make the trip with me, dear? We might be able to get a little shopping done as well."

"I'd like that."

"You had him in your sights and didn't shoot?" Farnsby clearly didn't understand.

"Carrie Sue was there with him. We couldn't take a chance on hitting her. Folks would have come unglued." Silbee didn't know why he was bothering to explain his actions to a man he considered a total weakling and a complete fool.

He looked appraisingly at the sheriff, watching the color come into his face and neck at the mention of Carrie Sue linked to the sheepherder in the same breath. He didn't know whether it was because Farnsby thought he still stood a chance with her, or because he was upset that she had humiliated him in front of the whole town. He just knew he enjoyed provoking the response in the man.

"Maybe watching him get his head blown off right in front of her is just what she needs to bring her back to her senses." Farnsby's voice was glum, and he held his beer mug in both hands, hunched over it as if he was afraid they would snatch it from him.

That told Silbee what he wanted to know. It meant Farnsby still thought that if the sheepherder was gone, he had a chance with Carrie Sue. He looked at the sheriff closely, weighing, calculating. If he thought that, he had to still think he had a chance at the Circle J through her.

Silbee was now sure that Farnsby had ambitions he was holding out from him. He was talking as if he had thrown in with them, but he was clearly trying to work both sides of the fence.

Two could play that game.

Silbee walked back over to the table where his men sat. Williams looked up as he approached. "You ready for me to get back out there and take another try at it?" Williams still took orders without question.

"Not yet. I don't think the time is right." His new evaluation of Farnsby deserved further thought. The next time they made a play on the sheepherder, they would be careful to see that it would fall on the sheriff's doorstep.

Uninvited, Farnsby came over to join them.

As he took a chair Silbee looked at him and said, "I'll tell you what I think. I think that sheepherder is a trouble-maker, and our local law enforcement oughta be riding closer herd on him. You need to take those deputies of yours and roust him around on a regular basis. Let him know how he stands with the law."

"I could do that."

"I don't think I'd take Cook if I were you. He's showing too many signs of having a conscience. Deputize a couple of them night riders to help you. They'd be mighty pleased to wear a badge and would do anything you wanted them to do."

Farnsby looked thoughtful. "That's not a bad idea. Cook is getting a little big for his britches."

"Mark my word, he'll run against you come next election."

"He wouldn't dare."

"I have a plan."

Audrey was glad to have Carrie Sue alone with her on the high seat of the big wagon. Paco followed in the

borrowed wagon behind them, out of earshot, particularly with the clatter the empty wagons were making.
Audrey had to raise her voice for Carrie Sue to hear,
even such a short distance away.

Carrie Sue looked at her in anticipation. "I had a feeling you did when you didn't send Jay for the sheep."

"That's just it. I'm not going to buy sheep."

That drew a surprised look. "What on earth are you
planning?"

"I'm going to buy calves. I didn't want Jay to know,
because down deep he still has the heart of a cowman. He
doesn't believe sheep and cattle can exist on the same
range. If I just bring them home, he won't have any choice
but to try it."

Carrie Sue had grown up on a cattle ranch, and the
concept didn't sit much better with her than it would
likely sit with Jay. And as to what her father and the other
ranchers would think of it, she shuddered to think. "Is this
wise? It'll be like throwing kerosene on a campfire."

Audrey smiled at her. "You don't believe it will work
either, do you?"

"Jay and Paco and the boys have all they can do trying
to handle the flock. Splitting them to watch a herd at the
same time is too much. They won't be able to do it."

"I have no intention of running a separate herd. I
was talking to a trainman on the eastbound awhile back.
You know they had a bunch of calves and sheep traveling in the same stock cars? He said they had no trouble
at all."

"That's penned up in a big rolling box. Out on the
range will be a different thing entirely."

A resolute look settled on Audrey's face. "I grant you I
don't think I could put cattle and sheep in a common

bunch. The cattle would continually try to get off by themselves or else they would try to drive the sheep away from them."

"There you go." Carrie Sue pointed at her. "That's exactly what I'm trying to say."

"But how about calves fresh off their mommas, how do they act?"

"Scared. Just like children would be without their mothers for the first time."

"I'm counting on that. I think if I turn some scared calves in with sheep that they'll want the security of having some other animals around them, even if they are a little different."

Carrie Sue was wavering but not convinced. "The sheep will run from them."

"I don't think so. When sheep are scared, or confused, or caught in almost any other situation you can name, their reaction is to band together. I think all they'll do is bunch up, calves or no calves."

"Could it work?"

"I think it could, and what would that show?"

"I suppose it would show that cattle and sheep could graze together."

"That's my plan."

Eighteen

I'm afraid trouble is gonna bust out over this sheep foolishness." Farnsby had his deputies, his force now swelled by three, gathered in the sheriff's office.

Deputy Cook eyed the newcomers suspiciously. "You sure we need this much help, Sheriff? There's been no trouble."

"And there's not going to be any now. I plan to see to that."

He looked at the deputy in a new light. It hadn't occurred to him that the man might be a Judas, patiently waiting to betray him. *If he is, Cook is biting off more than he's going to be able to chew.* "I intend to get a tight rein on things before trouble breaks out."

That could be a double-edged sword, and he knew it. Taking the new deputies out of town with him while leaving Cook to handle duties in Three Forks would put Cook in the public eye that much more. Farnsby would have to make a really good showing on handling the sheep situation or else this whole business could blow up right in his face. Of course, he could also make sure Cook didn't handle things all that well in his absence. That thought appealed to him. *We'll see who runs against who in the next election.*

He looked at the deputy. "I'll be depending on you to keep a lid on things in town while I'm out trying to keep things under control in the county."

"You know you can count on me, Sheriff."

Farnsby scrutinized the bland look on the deputy's face. *Was Silbee right?* This didn't look like a man with ulterior motives. If he was scheming behind his back, he was mighty good at hiding it.

Farnsby and his new deputies mounted their horses and rode slowly out of town. He motioned them up alongside him once he was out of sight of Three Forks. "You guys like the idea of wearing those badges?"

He got a chorus of enthusiastic responses.

"You want to keep them?"

Even more enthusiastic responses.

"All right, here's the thing. What I need is some bedrock loyal deputies. I'm going to share a secret with you. I think Deputy Cook is setting himself up to run against me next election. That kind of disloyalty is sad to see."

"Biting the hand that feeds him," one said with a scowl on his face.

The rest agreed in yet another chorus.

Farnsby smiled. He could teach this bunch to sing as a choir if he wanted.

"If you hear anything like that at all, I want you to get it to me as soon as you can. And in the meantime, anything I want him to know, I'll tell him myself. You understand what I'm saying? I don't want you guys telling him anything."

They all pledged themselves to secrecy.

"The other thing, I need deputies who aren't afraid to make things happen. A lot of people don't know that the letter of the law is for civilians. In order to make law work the way civilians need for it to work, lawmen sometimes have to stretch it a bit, and that comes with the badge. I need deputies that will do whatever I tell them to do, even if it looks like we *are* stretching things a bit."

They had no trouble with that concept.

They were the perfect henchmen for him; they hadn't had an original thought in years, if ever. He could do their thinking for them, and they would follow him blindly. That was the problem with the night raid; he had left it up to them to do the thinking and planning. He wouldn't make that mistake again.

He singled out one man and edged him over to the side. "Edgar, I've got a special job for you. I want you to stay behind. I need to know how good Cook is at his job. I want to set up a little test."

Edgar was properly awed by the responsibility, but he didn't understand.

"Test?"

"I want you to stir up a few things. Make some stuff happen around town."

He handed him some money. "Buy a bunch of drinks and try to get a good brawl going over at the Four Aces. Anything else you can think of that might be a good test of Cook's ability to handle trouble. Can you do that?"

"You can count on me, Sheriff." He thought a moment or two. "But what if I get caught?"

"You have my full protection. I'll tell people that it was a test, and you were doing it on my instructions."

A chance to get drunk and disorderly with immunity and cause trouble with impunity? This was too good to be true. Edgar spun his horse to ride back.

"But try not to get caught at it," Farnsby shouted at his back. "Right?"

"Like I said, Sheriff," he yelled over his shoulder. "You can count on me."

"Cows!" Jay was incredulous, not believing what his eyes were telling him. "You bought cows?"

Audrey gave Jay a couple of light pats on the arm. "Calm down, dear, I didn't buy cows, I bought some small calves."

"Didn't nobody tell you they grow up to be cows?"

He looked over at Paco and Carrie Sue. "How come you two let her do this?"

Paco shrugged. "She is the *patrona,* Señor, the boss. I follow her orders."

Jay shifted his gaze to Carrie Sue. "I know *you* don't follow orders."

"I agree with her," Carrie Sue said with a defiant look on her face.

He seemed totally exasperated. "You were raised on a ranch. You know sheep and cows can't share the same range."

"I believe that is what we are about to find out," Audrey said. "Paco, please unload them."

"No!" Jay threw his hat down on the ground. "There won't be no unloading. We can run them right back and get three times as many sheep for them."

"Trust me on this, son. They're here, and we have nothing to lose by seeing how they react with the sheep."

"Nothing but a hail of bullets when all the cowmen in the area ride down on us with vengeance in their heart."

He ran his hand through his hair in frustration. "The only thing I can think of worse to them than running sheep is running sheep and cows together."

"Why don't you go back to the house and splash some cool water on your face, maybe take a little pull off that jug we keep to make cough syrup."

"Are you saying you know you're driving me to drink?"

"No, dear, but if it would help settle you down, perhaps it'd be for a good cause."

He put his hat back on and tried to compose himself. "Well, what's done is done. Let's get them unloaded. I don't know how in the world we're going to handle two herds at once."

Carrie Sue brightened up, "Jay, your mother thinks that—"

Audrey silenced her with a hand on the arm. "Hush, dear, let the menfolk get on with their business. We'll see soon enough."

Jay and Paco rigged some planks and started leading the frightened calves down out of the wagons one at a time. As soon as they were on the ground they tried to run every which way, but Lady immediately got them in hand.

Jay smiled. "It don't appear to matter to Lady what kind of critters they are, she figures herding is herding."

"Maybe she knows something we don't, dear."

They got the calves down on the ground, and Paco headed off to return the borrowed wagon. "Now what?" Jay asked.

Audrey watched the little Border collie as she gazed at the group she had corralled, looked over to the flock farther down the meadow, then turned her head back to the calves. She seemed to feel the need to be in both places at once.

Audrey put a hand on Jay's back and pointed to the lumber. "I think you should load the planks back into the wagon and let me think on it for a moment or two."

Carrie Sue had also noticed the consternation of the little dog. She smiled. She knew exactly what Audrey was waiting for. Jay was too flustered to notice.

A couple of sheep broke free from the flock, and Lady took several quick steps to go get them. Then she stopped. As soon as she left, the calves began to head off as well. She only had one course open to her, and, just as Audrey had suspected, she began to drive the calves over to the flock of sheep.

Jay stepped down and removed his gloves. He pushed his hat back on his head. "What is that fool dog up to?"

"It would appear she can't watch two separate groups at once, dear. I think she's merely simplifying things."

"If she runs those calves over by the sheep, she's going to spread that flock ten ways from Sunday. It's going to take all of us to round them up. I wish you hadn't sent Paco back with that wagon. We're going to need it to take these critters back to town."

"Be patient, Jay. It's cows the sheep are afraid of, because they are so much bigger than they are. These calves aren't that big."

Lady drove the calves right up to the flock. As Jay had predicted, the sheep shied away. Jay watched in amazement as the sheep created a void between themselves and the calves. Then Lady circled the flock, using the sheep to create a wooly pen around the young bovines.

The calves understood what a pen was. Their heads went down, and they began to graze. When the calves began to graze, the sheep understood that they were no threat, and they went back to grazing as well.

"Well I'll be hog-tied." Jay scratched the back of his head.

"It would appear that Lady agrees with us, dear."

Jay was astonished. "Who would have guessed that the sheep would make a pen around the calves?"

"You missed the point, dear. The sheep didn't do it. Lady did it."

"I guess you're right at that, but don't forget they're still going to grow up to be cows, no getting around that."

Audrey's voice was controlled, patient. "No, I didn't forget that. They will grow so slowly that the sheep will be quite comfortable with them all the way. I don't think it will be a problem."

"The sheep will nibble the grass down so close that the cows won't be able to make a meal."

"I suppose that is what we are trying to find out, isn't it? I mean, everybody talks about that, but I don't know that anybody has ever tried to prove or disprove it. I think it's time someone did."

Nineteen

Amos, Judy, and Joseph neared their next stop, the town of Three Forks. They made night camp, and Judy looked across the fire at her husband. "I still don't understand how you know where we need to go next."

His love was clear on his face as Amos looked at her gentle features glowing in the light of the dancing flames of the fire. She wanted to be a good helpmate, but she had led too sheltered a life to fully understand his former out-law days.

"There are a lot of places I have to go to make amends. To make it right for how I used to treat people."

"You were such a rascal."

Joseph's sides heaved with silent laughter. "Rascal, that's one way of putting it. He was a purebred, dyed-in-the-wool sinner, girl. One of Old Scratch's frontline troops."

Amos grinned. "I'll admit the Devil took a licking the day Jesus claimed me for his own."

"Hello the fire," a voice called from the darkness.

Amos pulled his rifle within reach. "Come in, and welcome if you're peaceful." This was dangerous country, and even a man of the cloth had to be prepared to protect those in his care.

"I'm as peaceful as they come; that's why I'm riding at night." He stepped into the light, hands well away from his guns. He was a sandy-haired young cowboy with pleasant, boyish features.

He spotted Amos's clerical garb immediately. "Parson, is it? I'm Jack Walker." He spotted Judy and whipped his hat from his head. "Howdy, ma'am. I didn't see you there."

Introductions were made, and Judy poured a cup of coffee for the young man and set a bowl of stew in front of him. He ate like a starving wolf.

"Appears it's been awhile since your last meal," Amos said.

Jack muttered an affirmation around a mouthful of food, then cleared it with a prodigious swallow, followed by a sip of the scalding coffee.

"You on the run, son?" Amos said softly.

He nodded, then paused with the spoon halfway to his mouth to answer. "Kinda, but not from the law."

He had scarcely put the bite in his mouth when Amos said, "Jealous husband?"

Swallowing and laughing do not mix. Amos stepped over to thump Jack on the back as he tried to get control of himself. Finally he responded, "I wish that was it, Preacher, I surely do. Begging your pardon, ma'am."

Judy nodded. She liked this personable young cowboy.

Another sip of coffee got him under control. "I'm not running from trouble; I'm running because of it. You might want to consider changing your course, Preacher, because you're riding right straight for it."

"Three Forks?"

"That's it. They've got sheep in cow country, and you know what that means."

Amos nodded somberly. "I do indeed. So that's why God is nudging me in this direction."

"God wants you to go where trouble is?"

"It often seems that way. That's where I can be the most use."

"Why isn't the law stopping it?" Judy asked.

"The law is a whole lot of the trouble. Sheriff Farnsby seems to be making more trouble than he's heading off."

Amos looked thoughtful. "Farnsby, I remember him. A strutting bird of a sheriff."

"That's him all right, though here of late he hasn't exactly been himself. He's got something riding him hard, and I sure enough don't know what it might be."

"He won't be happy to see me." Amos looked embarrassed. "I did a few things before I put this collar on."

"Preacher, I got saved when I was just a button, but I reckon we all backslide from time to time. Reckon I didn't know preachers did it too."

"Preachers aren't anything but men. We've all got our weaknesses. So you think there's trouble coming, and you left because you didn't want to be part of it?"

"You pegged me when I first rode in, Preacher. I'm not a fighter; I'm a lover. Or would be if'n I had the chance."

He grinned at Judy again. "Begging your pardon again, ma'am."

Farnsby prepared his men for what he wanted them to do. "Mostly what we need to do is just make our presence known, make that sheepherder's life miserable."

He led his little band over the ridge to where he knew the sheep man had his smelly critters at the present time. "Well, would you look at that?"

The group reined up at the crest of the hill. They couldn't believe their eyes. Jay sat over to the side while Lady kept a watchful eye on a most unusual flock, or herd, or whatever it might be called.

"Sheep and cows together?" a deputy said. "I didn't think it could be done."

"That what you see?" Farnsby sneered. "I see a cattle rustler trying to hide his spoils in the middle of a bunch of sheep. Let's get him, boys." They rode down the slope.

Up on the ridge Williams looked up from the scope of his rifle. "I got him lined up, boss, but here comes that sheriff with some other people." The pair had come out to make another try at Jay.

"That sheepherder is plumb chuck full of luck. If it was just Farnsby, I'd say pull the trigger and we'd blame it on him, but it doesn't suit my purpose for him to have witnesses to say he didn't do it. It still ain't the right time. I don't know what it's going to take to put him down. Beats all I ever saw."

"What do you make of them sheep and cows together?"

"I'd say that is a right interesting concept. I've used the sheep in cattle country thing to stir people up, but I'm not as emotionally involved in it as all of these cow people around here are. It appears I may have to give it some thought when I take over the Circle J."

He spun his horse. "Well, we're going to do no good here now; let's go back."

They mounted and rode off as Farnsby and his men rode up to Jay.

"What are you boys doing out this way?" Jay asked. He took note of the badges on the chests of men he knew to be drunks and saloon dregs. That was not a good sign.

"Catching a rustler." Farnsby said.

"What'd you do with him?"

"We threw a rope over him, drug him to the nearest tree, and hung him." A rope snaked out, settled over Jay, and jerked him off his feet as he began to struggle.

On the ridge Audrey and Carrie Sue were headed back to the Bar-M in the wagon. Carrie Sue decided to turn and take one last look at Jay before they disappeared over the hill. She saw what was going on and screamed.

Audrey pulled up the team and looked back too, then turned the horses and whipped them into a run. Carrie Sue pulled the rifle out from under the seat and began to fire.

The sound of the gunshots stopped Silbee and Williams. They rode back up on the ridge to see what was going on. Down below they could see Farnsby and his men dragging Jay toward a tree, their intentions clear. A wagon was barreling down the hill. They could see puffs of smoke from the rifle Carrie Sue was firing. Then moments later, they could hear the sound of the shots.

"This is interesting." How to exploit this situation? The women would be sure to spoil the hanging. Silbee could see that. He could go ahead and shoot the sheepherder, but there would be no chance to pin it on anybody else. Then he knew what to do.

"Kill the sheriff."

He would let the sheepherder and his friends explain their way out of that one.

Williams stepped down from his saddle and pulled the rifle out of the scabbard. He lay down, braced the rifle on a rock, and took careful aim and one deep breath. Then he slowly squeezed off a round. Just as the powerful weapon recoiled, one of the deputies stepped in front of Farnsby and was hit right in the chest by the heavy-caliber bullet. He flew back as if hit by the kick of a mule.

"Again?" Williams asked.

"That does it. The plan won't work now," said Silbee. "Let's get out of here."

Down in the valley the deputies looked at the approaching wagon. One of them started to return fire, but Farnsby said, "Don't shoot, you knot-head. If we shoot up a couple of women, this whole countryside will be up in arms."

He dropped his rifle and held up his hands. The deputies followed suit.

The wagon rolled up, and Carrie Sue covered them with the rifle.

"What's the meaning of this?" Audrey asked.

"We caught Mendelson red-handed with all these calves," Farnsby explained. "We hang rustlers in these parts."

"Then we just saved your life."

"Huh?"

Audrey pulled a piece of paper from the pocket on her riding skirt. "If you had hung him, and I showed people this bill of sale for those calves, he wouldn't have been the only one hanging."

"Bill of sale?"

She handed it over for him to look at. One of the deputies began to untie Jay's hands. As soon as he was free, his first act wasn't to remove the noose from his neck, but to hit Farnsby square in the mouth. Farnsby went down hard; then Jay jerked the rope off.

"What kind of sheriff is it that hangs people first and hunts evidence later?" Jay was seriously angry, rubbing at his neck where the scratchy hemp rope had irritated it.

Farnsby raised up on one elbow, rubbing his bleeding mouth with the back of his hand. "Not so fast. I've got a dead deputy over here. I'll be taking Carrie Sue into custody."

Jay held up his hand, and Carrie Sue tossed him the rifle. "You won't be taking anybody anywhere."

He worked the lever far enough to ensure there was a shell in the chamber. "Besides that, you need to start using your eyes. Which way did the wagon come?"

"Down that slope." Farnsby indicated it with a nod of his head.

"Rifle shot knocked old Elmer back a good ways, didn't it?"

"Yes."

"Wouldn't that bullet have to make a mighty sharp turn to cause old Elmer to fly back that way, if it was her that shot him?"

Farnsby got to his feet, realization dawning on him like ice water thrown in his face on a frosty morning. "Somebody else was doing some shooting."

"Now you're getting it. And I figure it was intended for me or you. Nobody had any reason for Elmer to be dead. And the way you boys were holding me, I was a mighty easy target."

"That bullet was intended for me."

"You got that right."

"I really hadn't thought of running for sheriff," Cook told the storekeeper. "But Farnsby is out of control."

Several men gathered around him in the little store. "It was bad enough when he was just a lapdog for the colonel, got worse when he tried so hard to win the hand of Carrie Sue, but now that he has this obsession with the sheep-herder, he just isn't making any sense at all."

"You sure you could handle it?" Walton asked. "Things kinda got out of hand when the sheriff rode out and left it with you."

"It did, didn't it? I came to find out that Edgar was behind all of that. It was a setup deal to make me look bad."

"If that's the case, it sort of backfired on them, because you managed to get it all taken care of in spite of the fact that you were here alone."

"Thanks. I hope people figure that out."

"They'll figure it out when I get through spreading the word. As far as Farnsby goes, hiring those night riders as deputies was the last straw. Collectively that whole bunch doesn't have enough sense to pour water out of a boot with the instructions written on the heel. We have to do something about it, and we don't have to wait for elections. I'm going to call a meeting of the town council."

Cook strode over to the bank with an obvious confidence that hadn't been there before. He was so used to being a yes man for the sheriff that he hadn't thought about the fact that he didn't have to be anybody's flunky.

He had made up his mind. He would run for sheriff, and he'd put the law above anybody that might want to use it for his own purposes.

He walked through the door of the bank, removed his hat, and let his eyes adjust. Karl Freeman was the bank president, and he spotted Cook as soon as he entered. The deputy didn't do much business with the bank on his salary, so Freeman wondered if his presence meant trouble. He waved him over. "Is there some sort of problem, Deputy?"

"Not the kind you are worried about. I need your advice about something. Walton is trying to get me to run for sheriff. He said Farnsby is out of control, and he's talking about getting a special election called."

"Why tell me?"

"I'd never do it without your backing, sir."

"*My* backing? You need Blake Johnson's backing to be sheriff. It's always been that way."

"You ought to talk to Walton, sir. He thinks if the townspeople would pull together, I could be elected."

"That's an interesting notion, Cook. Maybe it is time we elected a sheriff who wasn't owned outright by one man."

Silbee and Williams rode back into the Circle J. Blake Johnson stood on the porch and eyed them suspiciously as they rode in.

I've overplayed my hand, Silbee thought as he caught the look on the colonel's face. He had let his usual unemotional countenance crack and had somehow telegraphed to Johnson the fact that things had changed. It was too early for that.

He thought he'd better repair that fence and take steps to allay any suspicion until he was ready to make his move.

He stepped down from the saddle and handed the reins to Williams. "You'd better take my horse. I gotta check in with the colonel." Williams raised an eyebrow at the use of the military title again, but he didn't say anything.

Silbee brushed trail dust off with his hat as he approached. Johnson had both hands in his front pockets, his coat was pulled back on either side, and he was puffing on the expensive cigar in his mouth.

Silbee didn't wait to be asked, but said, "We just come from checking up on the sheepherder, Colonel."

Johnson frowned. "You didn't hurt him, did you? I told Audrey I wouldn't let you hurt him."

Audrey? Silbee noticed that change immediately, as well as the implication of the promise the old man had made. Johnson was definitely going soft. But he could use this new development to his advantage.

"No, but when we saw him, the sheriff was about to hang him."

"Hang him?" Johnson jerked the cigar from his mouth, color rising in his cheeks. "I told that half-witted sheriff—"

Silbee put a hand on his arm. "It's all right, sir. Williams and I broke it up. We were a long way off, and I fear we killed his deputy in the process, but we stopped it."

The reestablishment of the military protocol did a lot to help Johnson regain his composure and feel more in control. "Very well, Sergeant. Fine work. I suppose I had better go deal with Farnsby."

Johnson turned and crossed the porch to go into the house. The use of the word "Sergeant" had grated on Silbee, but it was not the right time to say anything. He would be better off if he hadn't slipped the other day. He usually planned a campaign better than that. It was a tactical error, and he didn't make tactical errors.

"That's not all, sir."

Johnson stopped with his hand on the door and looked back, "There's more?"

"From where we were sitting, we could see Carrie Sue and Mrs. Mendelson coming to help him in a wagon. Carrie Sue was shooting a rifle at them."

Johnson laughed. "Yes, I'm sure she was."

"Colonel, I may be wrong, but I think the sheriff arrested her. It looked that way anyway."

Johnson took a couple of quick steps back toward him, his attention completely focused. "Arrested her? For what?"

"I don't know, sir."

"Why didn't you stop them?" His anger was clear on his face.

"We were too far away. Besides, we knew you were the one Farnsby answered to, not us. I thought the best course was to report to you as quickly as possible."

"You did the right thing. Have one of the men saddle my horse, would you, Sergeant?"

"Yes sir, right away."

"I'll have Farnsby's head for this."

Twenty

*F*arnsby rode into Three Forks just in time to see Cook coming out of the Wells Fargo office, stopping to shake hands with the station agent, Phil Daniels.

I should have known better than leave Cook a free hand here in town. I know what politicking looks like when I see it.

He rode over toward them, but the agent took one look at him, turned, and went inside. If Farnsby had any doubt that Cook was running for office, it was gone now.

He pulled up and crossed his hands on his saddle horn. "Tell me you ain't putting your name in the running for my job."

Cook hooked his hands in his suspenders, surprised that Farnsby knew. How could he know when he had only decided it himself a couple of hours ago?

"I hadn't given it a thought until today, but I'm thinking on it now. You've let all this stuff get to you, Sheriff. You ain't the same man you used to be."

Farnsby held out his hand. "Well, I ain't gonna pay you while you try to get my job. Gimme that badge."

"Figured you'd see it that way." Cook took off the star and tossed it to Farnsby.

"You're gonna get mighty hungry before election time rolls around."

"Not so hungry. The city council just voted to have a special election on Saturday. I can last three days. I figure I have at least that much credit over at the restaurant. This lets me politic full time, and with a clear conscience."

Farnsby watched the man walk away from him. *Three days! I've only been out of town a few hours, and already there's an election set. There's simply no way that—*

"Farnsby!"

The sheriff turned to see Colonel Johnson riding up. "Your office. Now!"

Farnsby turned his horse. He regretted being snippy to the colonel earlier. He would need him now more than ever. He had better do some of the best groveling of his life, and he'd better waste no time doing it.

Johnson entered the jail and went straight to the back. Farnsby hollered after him. "You looking for something, Colonel?"

Johnson came out of the cellblock, "If I'd found what I was looking for back in those cells, you'd be a dead man. I was told you had arrested my daughter."

"Have a seat, Colonel. I was afraid for a while I was going to have to. I had a deputy killed, and she was the only one I had seen doing any shooting. However, thanks to some shrewd figuring on my part, I saw it couldn't have been her gun that did it, what with the way the deputy fell."

"I'd have had that badge if you had done it."

Farnsby got a sour look on his face, "Seems like everybody is after my badge."

"What do you mean by that?"

"It seems they've called a special election for Saturday to vote on who ought to be sheriff."

"Without checking with me?" Johnson's temper flared. "What is going on around here?"

Johnson jumped up and stalked out of the jail.

Maybe there's hope for me yet, Farnsby thought.

The colonel wasn't happy with him right now, but he just might keep his job simply because the colonel didn't want anything happening that he hadn't decreed. This situation could work out to his advantage if he played his cards just exactly right.

Peyton didn't get it. "So how would it have helped the situation to shoot the sheriff? I thought you were going to pin it on him when we shot the sheepherder."

"It don't matter now since Frank missed the shot."

Williams grimaced. "Ain't my fault. That bullet was already in the air when that deputy stepped in front of it. I can't call them back, you know."

"I wasn't blaming you; it was just bad luck."

"I still don't get it." Peyton was like a dog gnawing a bone. Once he had something in his head, he wouldn't let go of it.

"It was an opportunity we couldn't afford to pass up. For my plan to work I gotta get rid of both the colonel and his brat of a daughter. I was ready to sacrifice my scapegoat to pin it on her. I think we still may have pulled it off even if we missed the shot at that pompous sheriff."

"You figure it'll work?"

"Can't see how it could miss."

"It can miss, and it did," a voice behind them said.

They turned to see Carter coming into the bunkhouse. "I just come from town. Farnsby told the colonel that he could tell Carrie Sue wasn't the one that done the shooting by the way the deputy fell."

"Rats!" Silbee flung the cartridge he had been toying with across the room, narrowly missing Carter. "Is nothing going to go the way I plan it?"

Carter sat down at the table with them. "How much does Farnsby being sheriff have to do with your plans?"

"How come you to say it like that?" Silbee heard the inflection in his voice.

"Because they got an election called for Saturday to decide who's gonna be sheriff, and the smart money says Farnsby ain't got a chance."

"Who'd run against him?"

"His deputy, Cook."

Silbee pondered the information. Things were changing fast, too fast. "That could be a problem. Cook is an honest man, and he thinks too much for his own good."

"Last I saw of the colonel, he was real mad about it being done without his say-so. He was headed over to the general store with blood in his eye."

"He may be mad enough at Farnsby to not fight it. Or he may be offended enough at the challenge to his power to back him in spite of it all. It could go either way."

Silbee sat thinking on the problem. The three knew to wait him out. Finally he said, "I think what is needed is a third candidate, one with the backing of all the ranchers in the valley. Hank, you ready to be the sheriff?"

"That what you want?"

"I think it is. Now all I have to do is convince the colonel that it's what he wants."

Silbee found the colonel in the restaurant. He walked up to the table, removed his hat, and said, "Sir, we need to talk."

Johnson dabbed at his lips with his napkin. "Sit down then. Have you eaten?"

"No sir."

Without asking, Johnson got the waitress's attention and gestured to duplicate his order for his guest, then turned his attention back to Silbee.

"Steaks, big ones. I presume that's all right?"

Silbee plopped his hat back on his head and straddled the chair. "Yes sir. I heard I was wrong about Carrie Sue being arrested."

"You just barely were. Apparently Farnsby was thinking about arresting her. I suppose it still looked that way at the time you came for me. You did the right thing."

The switch in Silbee's attitude didn't seem to register on the colonel at all. He simply accepted it. "Yes sir. I also hear there's an election for sheriff in the works."

"Confounded nuisance," he growled. "They didn't check with me at all."

The waitress brought the steaks. They were well done, the way cowmen liked them. People who nursed cattle for a living generally didn't want their beef rare. Each of the steaks completely covered the plate, with a big baked potato sitting in the middle of the meat.

Silbee turned the chair around and sat down, pulling up to the table.

"Ah, this looks good," Johnson said. "Anyway, I have no good way to go at all. I either keep that brainless sheriff, or I give in and let them elect one over which I have no control. Either way, I lose."

Silbee tucked his napkin in his collar. "There's another way to go, sir."

"How's that?" Johnson sawed off a big bite and put it into his mouth, chewing with satisfaction. "That's good beef."

"You remember Hank Peyton? He was a corporal in the regiment. He was a policeman in Saint Louis before the war."

Johnson paused with a bite in midair. "You don't say. I never knew that."

"He has the experience. He's a good man with a gun, and he's as tough as they come. You remember when we nearly got ambushed by them Yankee troops? Hank took his reins in his teeth and charged right at them. He broke up that ambush before we could even get a skirmish line formed."

"I remember. I put him in for a medal for that action as I recall. Did he ever get it?"

It was just like the colonel not even to know. "Yes sir, he did, and that'd look pretty good in an election campaign too. But best of all, Colonel, he's one of us; he'd be your man."

"Interesting. I could probably swing the votes of the cowboys and ranchers behind him, but would that be enough?"

"I think Cook will get a lot of votes from the townspeople, but there are still some people who would vote for Farnsby too. I figure if we put Peyton in the race, and got the ranchers to vote as a solid block, Farnsby would muddy the water enough to put him in."

"Well, well. I think I like that option. Eat your steak, Sergeant; it's getting cold."

Twenty-one

*I*t was as if the circus was in town. All three candidates bought drinks and glad-handed everyone in sight. Everywhere the townspeople looked they found both planned and impromptu political caucuses. Days were a constant succession of face-to-face meetings about the upcoming election. Nights were lit up by torchlight parades, and it was hard to accommodate three such events in a town that basically had only one street. Some of the resulting political discussions involved bare knuckles.

Johnson threw a party out at the Circle J for the area ranchers, who attended to a man. They stood around the study swirling brandy in stemmed glassware, an unfamiliar drink for most of them.

"We used to have our own sheriff, boys," Johnson said.

"We still do, only he's gone nuts," responded Tucker from the Angle Iron.

Johnson nodded. "Can't argue with you there. We aren't sure what caused Farnsby to lose his sanity. Seems to be a number of reasons. But the bottom line is it leaves us with three choices: We can leave our own man in office, but worry about what he might do in his mental state. We can allow the merchants to put a man in office who will in all practicality become a city marshal rather than a county sheriff. Or we can put another man in office who will answer to us."

Coulter from the Bar C said, "Guess we'd all rather have that last option, Colonel, but who would we back?"

"What if I told you I knew a man who rode with me in the war, was a decorated war hero, and used to be a peace officer in Saint Louis?"

"That sounds like a man I could back," Tucker said. "Who is he?"

"Hank Peyton."

Coulter frowned. "Peyton? Ain't he a gun slick?"

"Mr. Peyton *is* very proficient with a gun, I'll grant you that."

"And about as friendly as a rattlesnake," Tucker said.

"He is a hard man, no doubt. I think the times call for a hard man. And though he is not particularly friendly, I think that if you will ponder the situation you will realize he isn't *unfriendly* either. He just keeps his emotions to himself."

The colonel gave them a moment for that thought to register before he added, "Cook, on the other hand, is as friendly as a lapdog and has an open link between his brain and his mouth. If he thinks something, it just naturally falls right out into words."

Their support was reluctant. The idea of putting a man into public office they weren't comfortable with didn't feel right. Yet the colonel's logic seemed sound. Maybe they didn't have to like the man for him to do a good job.

Johnson played his trump card. "Best of all, he's a cowman to the bone. We could count on him doing right by us, and we know how he feels about smelly sheep on the range."

That closed the deal, and each man promised to go back and try to secure the votes of his ranch hands, usually a sure thing.

While the ranchers were meeting, Silbee was working with Peyton, trying to get him to growl less and smile more—though, when a man ran on a "tough enough to do the job" platform, a serious look didn't hurt anything.

"Tell me again why I want to do this nonsense?" Peyton was less than enthusiastic about running for office. "Biggest bunch of bull I ever saw."

Silbee was being unusually patient with the man. "Use your head, Hank. When we get rid of the colonel, we'll be sure the law won't get involved, because you'll be the law. Don't worry, I'll supplement the salary; you won't lose anything on the deal."

"Well, it ain't my kind of thing."

"You know, in a lot of towns the sheriff gets a piece of the action from the local saloon and gambling houses. That probably wouldn't be hard to set up here. You could end up a rich man if you did this right."

Peyton snorted. "I could end up a dead man if I did it wrong."

"Anything worthwhile has a risk involved, you know that."

"I ain't kissing no babies."

Over in the saloon, Farnsby was in his element. He liked to campaign, and it brought him back to his old self, flashing a bright smile sure to charm the ladies and putting out a ready line of blarney for the men. Since he had hired his new deputies he was the champion of the low-life individuals in the county. They never voted, but this time they would make an exception.

"You know me," he told those assembled. "Andy, you know what I stand for. We ain't had no killings during my term of office; in fact, it stays pretty peaceful around here."

He looked over to the saloonkeeper. "I've never stuck my nose into how you run this place, and I ain't never treated any of your customers bad."

"That's true, but it *is* common knowledge that you're the colonel's man."

"That ain't true at all. We're all pretty beholden to the ranchers around here to keep the economy alive, ain't that right? I try to keep them happy, particularly the colonel, but I've never done nothin' against the interests of the townspeople."

The saloonkeeper admitted he didn't know of any instance when Farnsby had sided against the townsfolk.

"Besides, it appears the colonel is backing Peyton for the job; that ought to make it pretty clear. All I know is, I have a good record, and I'm running on that record. You people need to vote for the name you know, and the man you trust."

Cook met with Wells Fargo station agent Phil Daniels, storekeeper Scott Walton, and county judge Jack Willoughby, in the general store. He did indeed have the businessmen and more solid townspeople behind him, but he was still worried, and with reason.

"I don't mean to carry tales, gentlemen," he said with a concerned look on his face. "But Farnsby plays fast and loose with the letter of the law. That bothered me the whole time I wore a badge with him. The law oughta be the law, it oughta be the same for everyone, and it ought not be for sale to the highest bidder."

"I think the highest bidder has bought him another man," Walton said.

"Yeah, Peyton seems to have the support of Johnson and the other ranchers. I figured after Farnsby pulled that stunt with the night riders that most folks were on to him, but he still has some popularity in parts of the community. I'm worried he may pull off enough votes to put Peyton into office."

"We'll just have to work to see that doesn't happen," the Wells Fargo agent said. "It's about time we had somebody honest in that office instead of a strutting bird that's always on public display."

Jay walked into the store to find the meeting in progress. The merchants didn't have the same attitude toward him as the cowmen had, but they were careful not to show support in public lest they offend those on the ranches.

The shopkeeper looked up. "Hello, Jay, you here for the meeting?"

"No, I've got a short list of supplies. I can wait."

"We're here supporting Cook for sheriff," Daniels said. "Who you backing?"

"Cook is a good man, and I can't abide either Farnsby or Peyton."

"Glad to hear it."

Jay stood there for a moment or two, obviously chewing something over. They waited him out. "You know, I have a man that works with me, Paco Gonzales. He lives out there with us now, but he still owns a little piece of property here in Three Forks. He'd vote for Cook if he had the chance."

Daniels said, "A Mex voting? Don't be ridiculous."

"Wait a minute, let's not be hasty here," Walton said. "Cook is very well respected with those people, and I don't think they like either one of the others at all. Judge, what's the law on this?"

The judge stroked his chin as he pondered. "Set me to thinking as soon as he said it. There are no provisions in our statutes limiting the vote to any certain nationality, provided the voters are male, of course. After all, we have German and Irish residents in the area, and they get to vote as long as they are property owners."

Walton smiled. "Most of the Mexicans hereabouts own property. Small to be sure, but it belongs to 'em."

They were quiet for some time before Jay said, "That's a lot of votes."

Walton nodded. "It's enough." Then he turned to Cook. "We can't tip our hand here. We have to try to line them up quietly, without letting the others know the move is in progress."

They stood in a tight little group, nodding and grinning. This was starting to make a lot of sense.

"I could get Paco to electioneer for Cook," Jay said. "Nobody would notice him doing it, and he could tell the other Mexicans why Cook wasn't coming himself."

"That's a good idea," Walton said. "The others will challenge it, you know."

"Of course they will," Daniels agreed, "but we already know how the judge will rule on that issue, do we not?"

Judge Willoughby smiled. "We do, indeed."

Twenty-two

I'd take it hard if you didn't support Peyton," the colonel told Walton. "I do a lot of business here, you know."

"Of course." Walton flashed an artificial smile. Fortunately nobody would know what happened inside a voting booth with the horse blanket curtain drawn. *Besides,* the storekeeper thought, *if you didn't buy your supplies from me, just where would you buy them?*

Johnson had twisted arms all over town. He was sure he had enough votes on the ranches to carry the election, but there was no point in taking chances. He moved down the boardwalk toward his next victim.

Daniels walked into the store behind him and looked at the rancher swaggering down the walk, puffing his cigar, his hands in his pockets. "He doesn't have a clue, does he?"

"No, I don't think he does," Walton said.

"How has Gonzales been doing?"

"I think he's going to be able to deliver close to a hundred votes."

"Who would have guessed?" Daniels got a pensive look on his face. "I just hope we aren't opening a can of worms that we'll regret later."

"If it becomes a problem, we can always get the statutes changed to rule it out. But you know what? I don't think it's going to be a problem. The Mexicans around here are pretty levelheaded folks as a rule."

"Tell me again what Paco is doing," Audrey said.

Jay couldn't restrain a grin. "He's lining up votes among his people for Cook for sheriff. He's doing very well with it."

"They can vote?"

"Apparently there is nothing in the statutes to prevent it as long as they are male and own property."

"Oh, that isn't right," Carrie Sue said.

That surprised him. "You don't think they should be able to vote?"

"It isn't that. It isn't fair that they should be able to vote and women can't."

"I agree, but that's a bigger issue than a local election. I think Congress is bare-knuckling that one out back in Washington right now."

"They've talked about it before."

"I hear tell some state back East has done it. Vermont, I think it was. It's coming."

"It's not coming any too soon." She bustled off, obviously very angry.

Jay looked at his mother. "Whew, I walked right into that one."

"Don't tell me; I'm on her side."

The election absorbed the people's attention to the point that they temporarily forgot about the sheep problem. Jay knew it was a temporary respite, but he welcomed it nonetheless. His help in swinging votes for Cook had won him support among the townspeople. The word hadn't gotten around about their range experiment, so things were going pretty well. He knew it wouldn't last.

He looked down at ... what was he supposed to call it, a flock or a herd? The animals were mostly sheep, so he supposed flock was still appropriate. They were no longer even segregating themselves but were grazing around the clearing with no regard for one another.

It was harder on Lady, since the calves were more adventuresome than their shaggy companions and often had to be coaxed back to the flock. It was a task she handled with an ease that gave no appearance of how vigilant she was required to be, or how quickly she had to be prepared to move at any moment.

Jay walked down among them. The calves didn't seem to be having any trouble finding graze. He knelt. The grass was tall enough that it was no problem, but getting close to a sheep that was eating he could see that it bit the grass off much lower than the calves. Still, this was green, fertile country. He just couldn't see how the difference in grazing could be the issue cattlemen wanted to make it out to be.

He walked through the flock. Yes, trouble would return. If either Farnsby or Peyton were elected, he could count on no help from the law. Cook knew of his support, and his role in marshaling votes down on the Mexican end of town. That might buy him some consideration. More than that, he felt that Cook was an honest man and would handle the law as fairly as he could.

What else could he do? Was there any way he could better protect the flock? Did he need to do anything to make the ranch more secure against attack? Surely he could do more than just sit around and be a target for whoever decided to ride against him.

He went over to sit on the hillside again. He couldn't pen the animals up, and he couldn't fence off the different areas of the ranch; they were constantly moving the animals from one grazing area to another.

The flock was most at risk when his young shepherds were handling them. Not that they weren't more than capable of handing the normal shepherd duties, but if armed men rode against them—well, he worried about that. They were under orders to run up into the trees if somebody rode against them, but boys might be boys.

I sure wish I'd never told them that David and Goliath story, he thought.

"He's under so much stress." Carrie Sue was worried about Jay.

"I know he is," Audrey said, "but I don't know what I can do about it. There are times I think it would have been best to sell the place to your daddy."

"You would have lived to regret it if you had; your heart wouldn't have been in it. We just have to help Jay all we can."

Audrey looked deadly serious. "That's just it; we aren't at equal risk. Nobody's going to risk hurting us. They figure if they get him out of the way, I'll have no choice but give in."

"Is that true?"

"No, that's where they don't understand. Even if they got rid of him, come hell or high water I'd still make this place work—just on principles. I'd never dishonor his memory—or his father's—by folding up."

Carrie Sue reached out to take her hand. "Then neither would I."

Audrey covered the hand with her own and smiled. "Jay is lucky to have you."

"Does he have me? We started talking a bit, but I don't know how he feels. I don't know how I stand with him." Carrie Sue tried not to dwell on the subject, but it was always there, always crowding the back of her mind, overshadowing even the danger and the problems they faced.

"You just have to be patient. Like I told you, it's hard for him."

"It's hard for me too, not knowing where I stand. I don't think he can hide behind that 'silent male' facade, or he shouldn't anyway. I know how I feel; why doesn't he?"

"I'll talk to him, dear. Maybe I can find out what's going on in his head."

Twenty-three

*T*he saloon closed during elections. Two voting booths had been rigged up in the back. All three candidates stood out on the porch doing last-minute electioneering and shooting hostile glances at one another. Each was dead certain he had it in the bag.

"Keep your people across the deadline until just before closing," Jay advised Paco. "If we show our hand too early, they could put together something to try and throw a scare into your people, maybe run them off. When it comes time, I'll go with you, and I figure several businessmen will too. There should be no trouble."

Ranchers and cowboys voted early, then with the saloon being closed, got back to work. It gave Peyton a lot of confidence. "The way I count noses, I've got this thing locked up. You concede early, Cook, and I might let you have your deputy post back."

"It does look like you're ahead, but I better play out the hand," Cook said.

"I don't know that your nose counting holds much water," Farnsby said. "A lot of the folks going in there have been personal friends of mine. I've always carried this election easily, and this time ain't gonna be no different."

"Those weren't your votes you're counting, Farnsby. Those were the colonel's votes, and they aren't coming to you this time. They're coming to me."

"We'll just see about that."

"We certainly will, in about an hour. Say, what's with all the Mexicans coming down the street. Today some sort of across-the-border holiday?"

Cook smiled. "I'd say they are coming to vote."

"*What*? That'll be a cold day in hell." Farnsby stepped in front of them as they got to the porch. "You people got no business here."

"Step aside, Farnsby," Jay said, "before I give you another licking."

"I'm still sheriff, and these people can't vote. It's against the law."

"Actually it isn't." Farnsby turned to see Judge Willoughby standing in the doorway. The judge smiled as he said, "The voting statute says all male property owners are entitled to vote. It says nothing about race or nationality. These men own property, so they are entitled to vote."

Jay shouldered Farnsby aside and led the group into the saloon. Farnsby looked over at Peyton. "We've been hoodwinked."

Peyton nodded. "The colonel ain't gonna like this a bit." He headed over to the hotel lobby to break the news to him.

"*Who* voted?" The colonel jumped to his feet, getting steadily redder in the face. He had been relaxing in the hotel lobby, waiting for the results to come in.

"The whole south end of town, I'd say," replied Peyton.

"That's against the law!" The colonel bit through his cigar, looked at it in disgust, and then threw it across the room.

"You know, I thought that too, but the judge said different. He said anybody that was a man and a property owner could vote, and them people all own some little shacks of some sort."

"I won't stand for this." Johnson began to pace back and forth across the hotel lobby.

Peyton knew he had to be especially careful when the colonel was in this kind of mood. "I don't mean to be uppity, but is there anything that can be done about it? It's writ right there in that law book."

"We can change the law book."

"Won't that be fixing the barn door after the cow is done gone? It won't change the outcome of the election."

Johnson stopped, distracted. "When will we hear those results?"

"Everybody seems to be over on the walk in front of the saloon slapping Cook on the back and shaking his hand. I'd say it was a pretty safe bet how the election's gonna come out."

Johnson fumed and sputtered for several minutes, gradually reducing in volume. Finally he seemed to force himself to relax. Taking deep breaths he pulled out another cigar and lit it. He drew down the points of his vest to straighten it, put his left hand in his pocket, and pulled himself together.

"Well, it won't accomplish anything for me to appear the sore loser now. I suppose I had better get over there and make a good show of being gracious. I just lost a lot of influence, but I can still start trying to build some bridges to get back what I can."

He crossed the street casually, as if he were out for an evening stroll. He walked up to Cook and stuck out his hand. "Sheriff, it would appear congratulations are in order."

"You don't say?" Cook was visibly surprised. "I figured you'd be sore."

"Sore? My goodness, no. The people have spoken. I spent far too many years defending the ideals of this country to be upset when democracy in action does not go my way. I assure you, my best wishes are quite real and very heartfelt."

"Say, that's mighty big of you, Colonel."

"Call me Blake; all of my friends do. Have a cigar?"

The grin on Jay's face seemed to light the kitchen of the small ranch house as much as the kerosene lantern. "I just wish you could have seen Farnsby's face when Paco and his friends walked up to vote," he told his mother and Carrie Sue. "He looked like he'd been roped and tied and somebody was coming for him with a branding iron."

"The only thing that would have been better would have been if the other ladies and I had been there, adding to the margin of victory." Carrie Sue was obviously still hot about that subject.

Jay shook his head. "Let's not go into that again. You have to know I agree with you there, and there's absolutely nothing I can do about it."

"I suppose not. How did Daddy take it?"

"Went over and congratulated Cook big as life. Gained a little respect in people's eyes there."

"How about Farnsby?" Audrey asked.

"Now that's a different story. I thought they were going to have to shoot him to get that badge off his chest. He's more than a little hot about them unexpected voters. He figures they stole the election from him. They couldn't make him believe that he only had a handful of votes at best."

Carrie Sue shook her head. "That's a shame. I've never thought much of him, but it used to be simply because he had more ego than any two men could carry. Now I think he really is losing his grip on his sanity."

"I'm afraid you're right. The man I watched ride off was a cannon primed to explode."

"Who does he blame for getting the Mexicans to vote?" Audrey asked.

"He knows I had the idea, and he knows Paco pulled the votes together. But I'm sure all his anger is aimed right square dab at me."

"He could be dangerous," Carrie Sue said. "You'll have to be more careful than ever."

"He *is* dangerous," Jay agreed. "But he was already aimed at me because of you. Nothing has changed."

"Because of me?"

Jay smiled. "He knows how much I like you, and I think he figures you like me too."

"Of course he does," Carrie Sue said. "I've made no secret of that. But how about this business of you liking me?"

"We need to talk about that."

Twenty-four

Where does this leave us, Rafe?" Peyton was back out at the Circle J.

Silbee shrugged. "No better, no worse. We got us an honest sheriff now, so we gotta be careful of him."

"I could take that sheriff out easy."

"No, that's your solution to everything. We can't shoot everybody that disagrees with us, and shooting an officer of the law would be pretty hard to ride around. It'll be better if we simply handled him. I think I'm back to my plan of using Farnsby as a whipping boy to take the blame for whatever we do."

"We may not have to." Peyton bit off the end a cigar and spit it onto the floor. He set a match to it and drew deeply. "I ain't never seen a man that mad before. He might get it done on his own."

"He might, but I don't think we can count on that. We need a strategy where we can be in control, where we can do what needs to be done and lay it right at his door."

Farnsby had a little shack up in the mountains. It used to belong to an old hermit, but after he died, Farnsby took it over, kept it stocked, and used it as a hideout when he needed to get out of town for one reason or another. When he was sheriff, there were some things it was just better he didn't see or know about.

He was every bit as mad as Jay had said. He hadn't been much before he got the sheriff's job, really nothing but one of the saloon derelicts he had always been so comfortable being around. Of course, that was not something he would ever admit to anyone, even himself.

In his mind, a month before the election he had everything: power, prestige, patronage of the most powerful man in the area, and the inside track to the most beautiful girl in the county. That didn't even count in the fact that he figured on someday owning the giant Circle J ranch, if he played his cards right.

He had had it all, and now he had ... what? ... a double handful of nothing. How had this happened? Where had he gone so wrong?

He ticked off the list in his head one item at a time. Mendelson had stolen the girl and his chance at the ranch. Mendelson's sheep had caused the crisis that had eventually cost him his job. It was even Mendelson who was behind the illegal votes that defeated him in the election.

All of it was Mendelson's doing, every last bit of it.

He'd leave the country. He'd go back East. But before he went, he'd square things with Mendelson.

But how? The sheeperder had nine lives. He had ridden down on him with a whole group of men, and somehow they had all not only been taken down, but also totally humiliated in the process. He had tried to frame him for cattle rustling, and the charge had bounced off him like water off a duck's back. Half the people in the county had tried to shoot the man, all to no avail. He had to think of something to get back at that sheepherder.

Where was the man vulnerable?

"Where did Farnsby go?" The colonel was back in his study at the Circle J. The question was aimed at Silbee.

"He left town like a scalded cat. He may not have quit running even yet."

Johnson shook his head. "I don't believe that. Farnsby is nothing if not petty. His entire life was his monumental ego. That's how I controlled him. It was the carrot and the stick. I built up his ego if he did what I wanted, and I tore it down if he didn't. He was acting crazy before the election. Now he's a loose charge of powder primed to blow. I'd feel better if I knew where he was and what he's up to."

"He's not blaming you."

"How can you be sure? I did withdraw my support from him and gave it to another man. I know how he thinks."

"I guess that's possible." That started the wheels rolling for Silbee. He didn't know why he hadn't thought of it before. He should spread the word that Farnsby was out there gunning for both Mendelson and the colonel. He could accomplish his ends, and Farnsby would be the perfect man to pin the blame on.

The colonel wasn't one to sit and wait for trouble. "We need to locate him. Round up everybody we can spare. I want them scouring the countryside."

"Yes sir, we'll get right on it."

Silbee went straight out to where his boys sat in the barn. On the payroll as gun hands, they didn't like to be out where the working hands were; there was too much chance they might have to actually do some work.

"We need to find Farnsby," Silbee said without preamble.

"I ain't too interested in being around him right now. I figure he's about to blow up all over somebody," Williams said.

"Exactly, and we want to make sure we control the explosion."

He looked over at Peyton. "Hank, you get back in town and be the gracious loser. Buy some drinks, but while you are at it spread the word that you're worried because Farnsby left town threatening Mendelson and the colonel."

"I didn't hear him say that, but it might be true."

"At least half of it is," Peyton said, "and I plan on seeing that it's all true. I also plan on him not surviving when he kills them."

"That sounds like a plan."

"Find him, and find him fast. Put him away, or kill him, whatever you have to do, but nobody is to see him, not now, not ever."

Audrey walked up behind Carrie Sue who was feeding the chickens. "Carrie Sue, why don't you make up with your father? He did the right thing about the sheep, and he was magnanimous about the election. I think he's coming around."

"Yes, you would think that, but I know him. If he doesn't get his way by running over you, he'll try charming you, and he's very good at it." She sprinkled the feed among the pecking birds absentmindedly.

"You think it's all an act?" Audrey sat down on the chopping block outside the chicken pen. The sun felt good on her shoulders.

"I've seen it before. I love Daddy, but I'm tired of his scheming and running over people. If he wants to make up with me, he knows where I am."

"I think he may have wanted to patch things up when he came over that day. He seemed to be looking for you, but you weren't here."

"Then why hasn't he been back?" Carrie Sue came out and closed the gate behind her.

"You know men, dear."

"Oh, I know men, especially two of them. Neither one of them will tell me how he feels. Both of them expect me to do it all, to bare my soul to them, then worry about whether my openness will be returned or not. That's not how it's supposed to work."

Audrey smiled at her young friend; everything was so personal to her. "So you're going to hold out until they come to you hat in hand?"

"No, I don't require that. But I don't think it's asking too much to be met halfway. Am I being unreasonable?"

"No dear, halfway is not asking too much." Audrey smiled. The colonel was not the only one who could be as stubborn as a mule. This young lady was not one to be subservient to any man, to wait quietly in the background until called on. She figured her place to be at her man's side, whether that man was her husband, her father, or her child. She was convinced that's how things ought to be out in this country—and maybe she was right.

Twenty-five

*T*he man rode slowly into town, the morning sun at his back. He was dressed all in black with a flat-brimmed, low-crowned hat on his head. His eyes took in the street from side to side without his head moving. The pistol at his side was not hidden by his jacket.

Walton was sweeping the boardwalk in front of his store. He saw the rider at some distance and wondered if one of the participants in the conflict had brought in a hired gun to set things right. The man had a look of resolution about him. Dread and fear swept through the storekeeper.

Then the man got close enough for him to see the clerical collar at his neck. He threw back his head and laughed. The man pulled up in front of the store. "I do something funny, friend?"

"No, Preacher, it's me. I don't know, at a distance I thought ... well, I thought you were a gunfighter coming to town, dressed all in black that way."

The preacher smiled. "A gunfighter, eh?"

Walton pointed. "Perhaps it was the gun. I didn't think a preacher would wear one."

"This is dangerous country, friend. Everything out here will poke you, sting you, claw you, or bite you. It's mainly for varmints. I cannot imagine a situation that would cause me to use it against a human being, not anymore."

"Not anymore?" The inflection on the words suggested there was more to it.

The newcomer got a funny look on his face. "I wasn't always a preacher, and trust me, I can use this gun."

The storekeeper stuck out his hand. "I'm Scott Walton, and this is my store. Step down. I have a fresh pot of coffee on the stove."

"Mighty neighborly of you." He took the hand and shook it. "I am Reverend Amos Taylor."

Amos dismounted, tied up his horse, which he called Biscuit-eater, and unbuckled the gun belt, putting it into his saddlebag. "I only wear it while out on the trail. I wasn't thinking clearly, or I wouldn't have still had it on. I know how it affects people to see me wearing it."

He followed Walton into the store. "One thing puzzles me, friend. Were you expecting to see a gunfighter ride into town?"

"It wouldn't surprise me at all. We have a bit of a situation here." The storekeeper gave him a weak smile. "Actually, we have several situations." He poured the coffee.

"Listening is a big part of my job." Amos sipped at the cup. It was good coffee, very good.

"It's sheep." Walton stepped back behind his counter and began straightening stock as he talked.

"In cattle country? I know how that is."

"It kinda spread from there. Our biggest rancher and his daughter are no longer speaking to one another. We've had repeated attempts on the life of the man running the sheep. We have a crazy ex-sheriff out running around trying to kill the sheepherder or the rancher or both. The whole town has chosen up sides. It's not a good situation."

Amos took a seat by the potbellied stove though it wasn't in use this time of year. "I suppose that's why God sent me here. I was riding in another direction when all of a sudden I got the strongest feeling I was supposed to ride this way. I don't discount those feelings, brother. I know when I'm being led."

"What can you do?"

"I don't know, but I'll know when it's the proper time. Will you spread the word that I shall conduct services on Sunday?"

"Oh, it ain't hard to get the word spread. Once it starts, it amazes me how fast things get around, as widespread as everybody is. Where are you going to have it?"

"I'm camped outside of town with my wife, Judy, and my friend and song leader, Joseph Washington. They are out there now setting up camp, and I came in to find a couple of men to help set up the tent."

"There are some across the street in the saloon if you can find two that are still sober enough to do it."

"Whadaya mean you can't find him?" Silbee said.

"Rafe, it's like Farnsby dropped off the face of the earth, "Peyton explained. "We asked around all those lowlifes that hang out at the saloon; that's about the only support he has left. We even roughed up a couple of them. They don't know anything, or they'd have spilled it."

Silbee pondered that. "Maybe he really did ride off, but somehow I can't believe it. I think he's just gone to ground. He'll show up. Did you spread the story like I told you?"

"Sure thing. Everybody in town is sure he's gone off the deep end and is trying to catch Mendelson and the colonel out where he can kill them."

"Everybody?" Silbee wanted it clear.

Peyton nodded. "Particularly the sheriff, just like you said."

"And what did he say?"

"He said it wasn't going to happen while he's the sheriff."

"Predictable. Entirely predictable."

"So," Peyton changed the subject, "are you ready for us to go over and try to catch Mendelson out in the open?"

"That time's coming up, but I think we need to set it up just a bit more. I'll let you know when to make your move. I do wish I had my hands on Farnsby though, or at least knew for sure where he is. Make it easier to set things up. Keep hunting him."

Johnson raised his eyebrows. "A preacher, you say? A real one?"

The ranch hand nodded. "A circuit rider, Colonel. He'll be having services in a tent on the edge of town."

"A tent meeting? Delightful! It's been a very long time since I've been to one of those. Thank you for telling me."

He watched the ranch hand disappear through the door. He had never gone to church services without either his wife or his daughter by his side. He missed Carrie Sue so much. If only she weren't so bullheaded. He resolved to make another try at reconciliation and called to the cowboy from the porch.

"Wilson, before you get back to work, could you hook up the buggy for me?" Perhaps Carrie Sue would consent to go for a ride with him.

As he approached the little spread, Carrie Sue and Audrey came out on the porch. He was in luck. She was there.

"Hello, Blake," Audrey said as he drove up to the house.

"Hello, Daddy," said Carrie Sue impassively.

He pulled up, tied the reins off on the brake, and then removed his hat. "Ladies. Beautiful day."

Audrey smiled. "It is indeed. Won't you come in? With nobody around but us, we're having a little tea, but I could put some coffee on."

"Tea? I haven't had tea in years. I think I would enjoy that."

His daughter was almost impossible to read. The corners of her mouth were up, but they stopped short of a smile. When she looked at him she seemed to be measuring, evaluating.

"There's a circuit rider in town," he said. "Carrie Sue, I've never gone to church without you or your mother. I wondered if you'd like to go."

"Of course, Daddy. I'd like that. Does the invitation extend to Audrey and Jay as well?"

Pushing. Always pushing. What would people think? Would they think he was condoning the sheep? He'd just have to deal with it. "Of course, dear. God's house is for everyone."

"God's house? Have I been away from town long enough that a church has been built?"

"No, it will be a tent meeting, but when God is there, it becomes his house. Am I not correct, Audrey?"

"That's how I look at it, Blake." She set out the blue-flowered cups and saucers and poured the hot tea into them.

Johnson tried a sip. "That's excellent." He gave Audrey a charming smile. "And will you do me the honor of going with me, Audrey?"

"I will, although I don't know about Jay." She settled into her chair. "The Gonzales family makes the ride down to the mission in Prospect on Sunday to attend mass. That leaves nobody to watch over the sheep if not Jay."

Perfect. He didn't mind Audrey coming along. Her presence would make it appear that he had nothing against her, but the boy was too closely identified with the sheep.

"Too bad," he said. "But I understand." He looked at his daughter. "Don't you wish to come home now, dear? It would be so much easier for you to get ready there."

"You think it's that easy, Daddy? You come in and make nice for a few minutes, and everything is supposed to be all right?"

"Everything isn't all right?" He worded it in his most innocent manner, avoiding her eyes by stirring a little milk into his cup.

"Are you ready to leave the sheep alone?"

"You know I can't do that."

Her voice became dismissive, withdrawn. "Then everything is not all right. I love you, Daddy, but I cannot

live in that house while you are taking action against
Audrey and Jay, no matter how nice you may be acting
toward them."

"I have nothing against either of them, Carrie Sue. It is
only the sheep I object to."

"I understand, and your invitation is a step in the right
direction. I will come with you to the service. Audrey has
said she will come as well. But I shall continue to stay
here in this house."

Twenty-six

Will you be all right while we are at church, Jay?"

Jay helped his mother up into the wagon. "Of course, Momma. I wish I could go with you. That's bound to cause some stir, you going with the colonel."

"We will meet him down at the crossroads and ride on in with him from there. Carrie Sue thinks he has a long way to go yet, but she thinks this is a move in the right direction."

"I'll have to see that to believe it." He moved around to help Carrie Sue up as well.

"We must go, but you keep your eye out for trouble, you hear?" Audrey said.

Carrie Sue looked back at him as they drove off. She worried about him so much.

At the crossroads Johnson suggested they transfer into his two-seat buggy. He pulled their wagon over into the trees and staked the team out to graze. "They'll be all right," he said.

When they entered the tent, the colonel with a lady on each arm, it caused exactly the stir that Jay had predicted.

"What does this mean, Blake?" Judge Willoughby asked him. "Are you making peace with the Mendelsons?"

Every ear was tuned to the answer. "It means we are friends, Judge, no matter how we may differ on what should or should not be grazing the range. I was hoping this would be a strong demonstration of that fact. I have never been in favor of the violence directed at these people, even if I do feel strongly that sheep do not belong on the range."

"Brother Amos, it appears that you are already doing some good," Walton said, "and you haven't even said a word yet."

"It isn't me, Brother Walton. When two or more gather in his name, he is present, and it is he who can do good."

The tent had been set up with the freight wagon across the end of it. Amos had figured this little arrangement out himself, and he was proud of it. The left hand sideboard of the wagon dropped down, and supports went under it to create a little stage. The pump organ was permanently mounted behind the drivers seat, and Judy played it from there. Benches erected from lumber in the wagon made it a very presentable little church.

The crowd was in place, and Amos stopped behind the stage to compose himself and pray. Judy stepped up and got the organ going. Joseph led the congregation in several well-known songs, his rich baritone voice ringing over the sound of the whole crowd, even above the organ.

All three of them counted on the setting, the familiar songs, and the organ making folks feel as if they were in a church.

Amos walked to the small podium and smiled. He put on some small half-glasses and opened his Bible. "I'm going to preach today on brotherly love and on the Great Shepherd."

There was a stir in the crowd. The reference to the word "Shepherd" caused many to expect a lecture on their attitude toward sheep. They weren't sure they wanted to hear it.

"It's just too good to pass up," Amos said. "You have such a perfect example right in front of your face. Have you paid any attention to those creatures out there that everyone is so upset about? They are timid, frightened creatures, and they are completely defenseless. Even rabbits have means of defending themselves by kicking, but not sheep. Their very lives depend on the shepherd."

Men in the audience squirmed, asking themselves why they had come here. Wives elbowed them to sit still, and the men remembered why they had come. It would have meant disaster in the households had they not come with their ladies by their side.

"We are no different," Amos went on. "We are defenseless except for the Good Shepherd."

Johnson spoke up. "Preacher, you are misinformed. One thing I am certainly not is defenseless." All over the room male voices agreed with him.

Amos closed the distance to the rancher. "Against sin you are defenseless, sir. Do you think your money will get you into heaven? Do you think all of the power and prestige you have here on earth will mean anything when you stand before the great white throne judgment?"

Johnson flushed red. "Well, of course not."

Amos moved back out into the center of the aisle. "The Bible says, 'The wages of sin is death; but the gift of God is eternal life through Jesus Christ our Lord.' If you want to look that up, it's Romans, chapter six, verse twenty-three. That means none of us are without sin, and if we are sinful we cannot hope to get into heaven. But Jesus paid the price for our sin on the cross, and because of him we have eternal life. Just like those sheep, we are dependent on the shepherd."

From that point Brother Amos launched into the theme of "love thy neighbour as thyself," tying in a little forgiveness, encouraging his listeners to heal the wounds that were so prevalent in the community. He caught a sideways glance here and there. He knew it was going to take more than one sermon to get the job done in that divided community.

After the service had ended and the people had left, he looked out at the empty seats. *At least they didn't seem to recognize me,* he thought. *Maybe for the time being it's better that way.*

Jay and Lady moved the flock onto new grass. It was a casual process, no point in getting in any hurry. He wasn't being as vigilant as he had promised his mother and Carrie Sue he would be, or he would have noticed the furtive shadow up on the hillside.

"There he is," Farnsby muttered. The former sheriff looked bad: beard stubble covering his face, still wearing the same clothes he had on when he left town, now much the worse for wear. He was downwind or Lady would surely have smelled the stench he gave off. There was little semblance of the man he had once been.

He was obsessed by the desire to kill the man below who had brought about his downfall.

He inched closer, tree by tree. "Whoops," he said and dropped down as he saw the dog's head come up. "I guess this is as close as that dog is gonna let me get."

He constantly talked aloud to himself now. He crawled over to a log and rested the barrel of the rifle on it.

A low growl emitted from Lady's throat. "What is it, girl? Somebody out there?"

Jay scanned the hillside but saw nothing. Still, Lady did not give casual warnings. If she indicated that something was out there, he could take it to the bank. He walked toward his pack to pick up his Winchester.

"Look at that. He's walking right toward me. It ain't gonna get no better than this." He sighted the weapon dead center on Jay's chest. He paused to wipe sweat from his eye, resighted dead center, and pulled the trigger. The rifle bucked in his hands.

Jay leaned over to pick up his rifle and heard an angry hornet pass overhead, followed by the report of a rifle. He dropped down behind his saddle, quickly spotting the puff of smoke on the hill.

Farnsby cursed and levered the rifle, throwing another shot after the first one.

Dirt kicked up in front of the saddle, and Jay shouldered his rifle and responded. The two exchanged several shots before Farnsby decided his plan wasn't going to work out. "That's the hardest man to potshot I ever saw."

"This ain't over," he promised as he ran over the hill to his horse.

Jay saw him go and sent a couple of ineffective shots after him. Lady started after Farnsby, but Jay shouted to stop her. "Let him go, girl. The last thing I need is for you to get shot again."

The sound of a horse startled him, and he spun to face a new enemy. It was no enemy; it was Carrie Sue. "I heard gunfire," she said, rifle in hand.

"Take it down a notch; whoever it was has gone away. If it hadn't been for Lady I'd be taking a dirt nap by now though."

Carrie Sue bent down to ruffle the dog's hair on either side of her head, looking her right in the face as she talked. "Good girl, I owe you a big one."

"*You* owe her?" He grinned. "It was *my* life she saved."

Her chin came up as she ignored the sarcasm in his voice. "Don't be silly. You know how things are."

Jay felt a little uncomfortable and changed the subject. "How was church?"

"Interesting. The preacher preached on sheep, people as a flock, and the Good Shepherd."

"Sheep and shepherds?" He laughed. "Sure would like to have heard that sermon. I'll bet it really ruffled some feathers."

"There were a few squirming as if they had on hair shirts, but nobody said anything, of course."

Jay wished he could have seen that response. "How did they react to Momma being with you two?"

"Daddy made this little talk about how he hoped this would make them understand that his opposition to sheep had nothing to do with you as people and that he didn't want to see any more violence directed at you."

"Given what just happened, it must not have done much good."

"I doubt that whoever shot at you could have been in the service and gotten here this quick."

"You did."

"I suppose that's true. You have any idea who it was?"

"I figure it was Farnsby, but I didn't get a look at him."

Twenty-seven

*F*arnsby emitted a steady stream of profanity all the way back to his hidden cabin, continuing as he went inside. *Life is not fair; the man is impossible to kill.*

The inside of the cabin looked like a garbage dump, even after such a short time. For a man who had been so vain about his appearance, and so concerned about how people viewed him, there seemed little vestige of that pride left.

He rummaged through pots, pans, dishes, and open airtight containers looking for something to eat. He finally found a pot with some beans in it. He tried a tentative sniff and turned up his nose. He tried a bite, found it not too objectionable, and sat down to devour the remainder of it.

His ambush hadn't gone well at all. He needed a new plan. Not only did he need Mendelson alone, he needed him without that accursed dog by his side. He needed to start watching the Bar-M and wait for him to go to town. He'd find a suitable ambush site on the way to town and waylay him there.

He had time. It wasn't as if he were going anywhere, at least not until he had accomplished what he set out to do.

"I heard in town that somebody tried to get Mendelson." Williams had just ridden back to the Circle J. He reported to Silbee first thing.

Silbee frowned. "Tried? I suppose that means they weren't successful?"

"Nope. That jasper has more lives than a cat. We've all tried to back shoot him and nobody is getting it done."

"It had to be Farnsby. I guess we know now he's still around. I figured he was. I wonder why we can't find him?"

Williams frowned. "I don't know. The boys and I have combed this country like currying a horse, and we ain't seen hide nor hair of him."

"Well, let's keep looking," Silbee said. "But now that we're sure he's around, we can proceed with plans to get rid of Mendelson and the colonel. Now that I'm sure Farnsby is here to pin it on."

Peyton cleared his throat to get their attention. "You guys hold it down; the colonel's coming."

Johnson entered the cookhouse. *These friends of Silbee never seem to be out doing any work.* "Why are you men always sitting around," he said. "I'm not paying you to warm your backsides all the time."

He looked over at Silbee. "It looks to me like these men are on the payroll as gun hands. I never authorized that. Either put them to work or send them on their way."

Peyton half rose from his chair, but Silbee stopped him. Wouldn't do to act prematurely.

The colonel changed the subject. "I just heard from one of the hands that somebody tried to shoot Mendelson."

"That's what Frank was just telling me," Silbee said blandly.

Johnson's eyes issued a challenge. "He came to tell you such news before bringing it to me?"

"I was just telling him that," Silbee said. "I told him he should've followed the chain of command. He should've told you first."

"Fortunately he wasn't the only one coming back from town, but let's watch that in the future, Williams."

"Yes sir." Williams said halfheartedly.

"Am I safe in assuming that we had nothing to do with this attempt?" He addressed the question to Silbee.

"Yes sir, you are safe in that assumption," Silbee said. "We understand that you said no violence was to be directed at those people."

"That was an order. It had better be understood."

Silbee worked hard at keeping the disdain off his face. "How do we go about discouraging those people about the sheep if we don't roust somebody?"

"I've been thinking about that, Sergeant. I think we will put an expeditionary force together, and we will go steal that herd. We'll take them off somewhere that they can't be found and kill the smelly things."

He paused and nodded, sure he had come up with the correct solution. "I think the perfect time would be when the young boys are watching it. They aren't armed, so they can be subdued and tied up without being harmed. That should make Mrs. Mendelson more agreeable when I come to make an offer for her ranch."

"That's a good plan, sir."

But there won't be any shooting of sheep, Silbee thought. *I'll take them off and sell the whole bunch and pocket the money. Or I'll wait and stock this range with sheep and cows both after I take over. Nobody else has bothered to notice that the sheepherder has proven cows and sheep can get along together, but I sure enough noticed it.*

Walton looked at the figure coming down the street: bearded, dirty, clothes ruined beyond recognition. "Is that Farnsby?" he said to Amos. They had been standing out on the boardwalk talking.

"Farnsby? The sheriff?" Amos asked.

"The former sheriff. He looks terrible."

Amos nodded. "I'd have to say he looks as if he has fallen on hard times all right."

Farnsby stopped in front of them, but seemed not even to see them. "Mendelson," he yelled at the store. "Mendelson, I know you are in there."

Amos spoke quietly to the storekeeper. "Is this Mendelson in there?"

"Yes."

"Then go keep him in there. I believe this gentleman and I need to talk." He stepped over and pulled his pistol from his saddlebag to strap it on. He flashed an embarrassed grin at the shopkeeper. "I fear your former sheriff may need something to think about to distract him from his hate."

Farnsby swayed on his feet and tried to focus on the store, oblivious to the activity off to his left. "Mendelson, come out here if you have the nerve to face me."

Amos took several steps and turned to stop right in front of the man. "Mister Farnsby, my name is Amos Taylor; most call me Brother Amos."

"You ain't my brother, Preacher." It was obvious he was too far gone to remember that he had seen Amos before. "You'd best step out of the way, because it may get to be a little hard to stay alive out here in a minute. Mendelson!"

"Mr. Mendelson has been asked to stay inside to give me time to talk with you."

Farnsby smirked. "I got no need to talk to a Bible-thumper. If he ain't coming out, I'm going in after him."

"I can't let you do that."

Farnsby sneered. "And just how is it you figure to stop me?"

Amos tucked his coattail back behind him to reveal the sleek Navy Colt. "Trust me, Mr. Farnsby, I can stop you. Neither of us wants that."

That startled him. "A preacher threatening a man with a gun? That ain't right."

"Through the years many of God's servants have been called upon to take up a sword in his work. He will guide my hand."

"This ain't right," Farnsby repeated. "That sheepherder took everything I had from me: my girl, my job, my pride, everything."

Amos kept his voice soft and even. "If that's all you lost, and it was all you had, you have a much greater problem than the man you seek."

"I don't understand."

"We all have trouble, Mr. Farnsby. No one is exempt. Even Christians have trouble. God doesn't promise otherwise. But a person's faith is something no one can take away, no matter what might happen to him."

"I don't believe you'll use that gun."

"Before I turned to Jesus, I made my living with this gun. I'll use it if you make me, and you must believe me when I tell you that you won't have a chance if I do. No brag, just fact. Didn't you understand a single word I just said?"

Farnsby snorted. "I heard you."

"If you try me on for size, or even try Mendelson, what happens?"

"One of us will be dead." Farnsby said it as if he didn't care which.

"And if it's you?"

Farnsby features hardened. "I couldn't be any worse off than I am."

"That just isn't true. Do you believe in heaven?"

His face changed. "I'd like to. I'd like to think my mother is there."

"If you believe in heaven, then you have to also believe in hell, for one cannot exist without the other."

"I'd more readily believe in hell than heaven. In fact, I ain't sure I'm not already there."

Amos shook his head. "Oh, you'd know it if you were there. It's a place of unbelievable torment. Not like doing a ten-year stretch in prison either. There's no getting out, no parole, no time off for good behavior, and no escape. If you don't go to heaven, you go to hell, and hell is forever. That's the toughest sentence a man can draw."

"You're just trying to scare me, Preacher. You saying I don't get past you to settle up with Mendelson?"

"I am."

"And if I draw on you, you'll win?"

"I will."

"That ain't right."

"You said it."

Farnsby seemed to puzzle over the situation, as if thinking was very hard to do. "You're also saying if I had this faith thing that you're talking about that things would look a lot better?"

"Even more than that. You can either die here in the street or get a chance at immeasurable happiness. It's your choice. It's always been your choice."

Farnsby shook his head violently. "I reckon it's too late for that. I've made my play. Everybody is looking."

"Are you willing to die because of what somebody might think of you?" Amos looked at him in disbelief. "I've got news for you. The way you look now, nobody thinks much of you anyway. They all think you have gone over the edge. Wouldn't you like to turn that opinion around? Wouldn't you like people to look at you without pity in their eyes again?"

Farnsby was confused; he didn't know what to think. He looked around. The street was full of people watching. "I used to be a big man around here," he said wistfully.

"No, you used to have people fooled into *thinking* you were a big man, but now you have a chance to really be a big man. None of us can ever become all we are capable of without God's help."

Farnsby's voice became small. "I've never bought into all that stuff."

Amos nodded. "I know, or you wouldn't be so completely defeated by a couple of simple setbacks. So, what's it to be?"

Time froze. Amos stood firm, not threatening, but managing to convey a complete confidence in the outcome if Farnsby made his play. Farnsby was convinced. Perspiration ran down his forehead.

Amos smiled. He knew he had him. "You need to pull that gun now. Use your left hand, and drop it into the street."

Farnsby did as he was told, dropping the pistol into the dirt.

Amos stepped down and put his hand on Farnsby's shoulder. "You've taken the first step. Let's go out to my camp where we can talk, and I'll help you get the rest of the way."

Twenty-eight

Judy looked up as Amos returned to camp. The man he had with him looked derelict, haunted. Amos introduced Farnsby to her, then to Joseph. Farnsby held out his hand. "Joseph is blind; he doesn't see it."

"I'm sorry."

"No way for you to know."

Then to Judy and Joseph, he said, "Mr. Farnsby is dealing with a few things right now."

"Nice to meet you, Mr. Farnsby," Judy said. "I was just about to make something to eat; will you join us?"

Farnsby didn't know how to respond, but she took his silence as a yes. She moved off to prepare the meal. "I'll help," Joseph said. They always set up the campsite exactly the same way, even measuring the distances, so he had no trouble navigating within its confines.

Farnsby looked after them. "Nice lady."

"Best thing that ever happened to me, friend. Have a seat."

They sat on logs by the fire. Farnsby said, "I don't know why I'm here."

"You're here because God is dealing with you."

"How would I know that?" Something was happening to him, he could feel it, but he didn't understand what.

"Because you are listening. Because when I told you that faith could change your life I saw a spark of hope in your eyes. I know the look; I used to be where you are. I was a scoundrel, stealing and cheating everyone I came into contact with. Someone told me Jesus loved me and would help me, but I figured it was far too late. You just said the same thing to me."

"I've done some bad stuff." Farnsby sat with his head in his hands, elbows on his knees.

"No worse than I have, and God not only forgave me, he turned my life around and is using it now for his purposes. He sent me here, and I think he may have sent me for you. I feel like you have sunk about as deep as you can go. There is no way to go now but up."

"You got that right."

Amos put his hand on Farnsby's shoulder. "But I sense you really do want to turn your life around and would take help if it was offered."

His head came up. "I need help ... and I'm here."

Amos started reading Bible passages to him, showing him the words as he read. He showed him how a blood sacrifice had always been required for sin to be forgiven and how only someone as pure as Jesus could make such a sacrifice sufficient to cover the sins of the world. He walked him through the crucifixion and the resurrection.

Farnsby was stunned. "You saying Jesus did that for me?"

"He did it for us all, and it most certainly included you. Do you believe what I've been telling you? Do you accept that it's true?"

"Yes, I do. I'll be switched, I really do." His eyes became bright, his face animated.

"All you have to do is pray to God and admit you are a sinner, then ask Jesus to come into your heart."

"That's it? That can't be all."

Amos moved over to put his hand on Farnsby's shoulder. "It is."

"It can't be; that's too easy."

"It would have to be much, much more if we somehow had to obtain our own salvation, but that's just it. We could never earn it out of our own works or our own virtue. It isn't what *we* do, but what Jesus did. It's a gift, a gift of grace. We aren't saved because we deserve it, but because of his love for us."

Farnsby went to his knees, crying. Amos led him in the sinner's prayer. When he finished, Amos said, "Congratulations, Brother Ron, you are a child of the King. If it is real, you'll feel different. You'll want to tell people. You'll want to be baptized as a demonstration of your faith. Most of all, you'll want God to start being the center of your life."

"Yes, yes, I want all of that and more."

"Then we need to get you baptized."

He looked down at his tattered clothes. "Let me go clean up first. I'd be embarrassed to offer a filthy body like this one to the Lord."

"Good idea. God would take you just as you are, but I'm sure he approves of the reasoning behind what you propose."

Judy came back. "How are you men doing?"

"Judy, meet Brother Ron. He's a brand-new Christian."

She broke out into a dazzling smile. "Wonderful." She tried to give him a hug, but he pulled back.

"Don't, I'm filthy."

"No, you are the cleanest you have ever been. Your physical body could use a little work though. You do know that right now as we speak, all the angels in heaven are celebrating, don't you?"

"I've sure got a lot to learn."

Amos slapped him on the back. "You will, brother, you will. Now go get cleaned up and come back to take supper with us before the services tonight."

Brother Ron still had clothes in his room at the hotel, or they would be stored if the hotel clerk no longer held his room for him. He crossed the street to find them as Jay stepped out from the restaurant next door. Walton was with him, and he looked up and said, "He's back."

Jay handed the packages he was carrying to Walton to hold and thumbed the strap off his pistol. "I guess I've got it to do."

Brother Ron stopped, and they looked at one another. Jay stepped down into the street and walked to the middle of it. The former sheriff smiled, opened his coat to show that he wasn't armed, and said, "You may find this hard to believe, but I just gave my heart to Jesus."

"This ain't some kind of trick?" Jay couldn't believe it.

Brother Ron was radiant. "That's what I've been asking myself the past couple of hours, but the answer keeps coming up the same. It's no trick; it's for real."

He walked closer. "I owe you an apology. I've been blaming you for everything, and it isn't you, it's me. Carrie

Sue didn't love me, but instead of understanding that, it was easier to blame you. When I started acting strange, people were afraid to have me as sheriff, and I blamed you for that too. It's all my fault, every bit of it."

Jay closed the remaining distance and offered his hand. "It takes a big man to say that."

Brother Ron shook the hand and shook his head at the same time. "Actually it takes a very small man, so small he finally hit bottom and had to be picked back up by the Lord."

"Looks like a big man to me, however you got there. Much bigger than when you were sporting that badge."

"In just a few minutes what you see will be much more presentable. I'm going to be baptized later, and I'd like it very much if you came."

"I'd like that, and I'll go get Carrie Sue and Momma. I think they'd like to be there too."

Brother Ron looked at all of the people watching them. They had probably heard all of it, but he wanted to be sure.

"In case you didn't hear," he shouted, "I'm a new Christian, and I'd like all of you to come see me get baptized at the church services tonight. I'm going to be a completely different man from now on, and I want you all to know why."

Twenty-nine

*J*ay returned to the Bar-M to find Colonel Johnson sitting at the table visiting with his mother, laughing and drinking tea. He seemed to be coming by more and more these days. "Colonel, what are you doing here?"

"I was out riding and decided I had better stop and check on Carrie Sue. I haven't given up on persuading her to return home, but we seem to still have one sticking point."

"The sheep?" Jay knew that issue surely hadn't changed.

"The sheep."

"Well, I'm glad that you and Momma have managed to become friends in spite of being unable to resolve that little problem."

"There never has been anything personal in it, son. It's all about range management." The colonel *looked* sincere; it was so hard for Jay to tell these days.

"It felt pretty personal to me when your foreman and those hard cases he runs with beat me up."

"Yes, well, er ... ah ... sorry about that, but I assure you they were *not* acting on my orders."

"If you say so."

Jay turned to the ladies. "Hey, do I ever have news. Farnsby has gotten religion. He came up to me on the street and apologized to me for the way he has acted. He's being baptized at the church services tonight and wants us to all be there. I told him I'd come, but I wanted to come see if you all wanted to go too."

Both ladies immediately said they did wish to be there. "Is this something I might intrude on?" the colonel asked. "I have my buggy and would count it an honor to be able to drive you into town. You too, Jay; I think I would like to see this miracle for myself."

"We'd be delighted, Blake," Audrey said. "Give us time to change."

Blake? Jay wondered what was going on. Maybe the colonel had changed tactics and was trying to get hold of the Bar-M through his mother. This situation would bear watching.

The services were nice. Later they were adjourned to the stream where Amos baptized Brother Ron, and it was all he could do to get him back up out of the water. The ride home was ... interesting.

Audrey and the colonel sat in the front, talking and laughing. Their voices carried to the back, but not clearly enough that the words could be understood above the thunder of the hooves of the team and the rattle of the wheels and rigging.

"Does this feel as weird to you as it does to me?" Jay asked.

Carrie Sue leaned close to be heard. "You mean does it feel like my father and your mother are courting at the same time we are? That's exactly how it feels."

"How do you feel about that?"

"Uncomfortable. But they both need someone. I can't see anybody replacing my mother, but I haven't seen Daddy this happy in a long time."

"Same here. No offense, but I've sorta been thinking of the colonel as the enemy, and the thought of him and my mother kinda grates on me. Like you said, nobody can replace my father, but you're right, I ain't seen Momma this happy in a long time."

Carrie Sue studied his face. "If they're serious, what does that do to things?"

He looked at her for a long moment, then seemed to make up his mind. "I'm going to ask him what his intentions are. If they did get together, well, that boggles the mind."

"You'd get the Bar-M."

"Would I? Or would the Circle J just get that much bigger?"

She frowned. "You think he's just after her ranch?"

"It crossed my mind. I think I'll ask him that too."

"I'd have to move back home. I couldn't stay at the Bar-M without your mother there to chaperone."

"Not necessarily."

"Oh Jay, why don't you ever say what you think? Why do I have to try and guess everything that goes on in your head?"

"I have nothing to offer you or I'd ask you to stay permanently. I do love you, I know that, but all I have is the clothes on my back if I don't get that ranch."

There it was. He hadn't said it before. She wanted to hear it again. "Can we back up and go over that again?"

"About only having the clothes on my back unless I get the ranch?"

"No, further back. I thought I heard something in there I haven't heard you say before."

Jay flashed a big grin, but she thought in the dim light that he also colored a little darker. "Oh, girl, don't you know I love you? I guess I have most of my life."

"What I might know and what you tell me aren't the same thing. A girl likes to be told, and told often. And I don't care what your prospects are, as long as we are together."

When the buggy pulled up to the house, Audrey invited Blake in for tea. The four of them settled around the table as she poured.

"Tea, huh?" Jay said. "I'll try anything once."

Audrey smiled. "Put a little sugar in it, dear. I think you'll like it better."

He put sugar in it and tried a sip. "Not bad. Still rather have coffee, but it's something different."

He shifted his attention to Johnson. "I don't know how to say this without feeling like I'm trying to be Momma's daddy, which I guess would make me my own grandfather"—he shook his head, trying to sort it out—"but I feel like I need to ask you what your intentions are."

Johnson threw back his head and laughed.

"You find that funny?"

"Of course it's funny, but on the way out here we talked about the fact that you two were probably wondering that very thing. I went further and said I bet you thought I was trying to get control of the Bar-M through your mother."

"It crossed my mind."

"Of course it did," Johnson said. "Look, I do love your mother, and I asked her to marry me on the way back out."

"Daddy! Without even warning me?" Carrie Sue looked stunned.

"She hasn't given me an answer. She said that we had to talk to you two first, but ..." he gave Jay a mischievous look "... but shouldn't I be asking you the same question?"

It was Jay's turn to laugh. "Funny, we talked about that on the way out too."

"It looks like it was a very productive trip for both of us. What did you decide?"

"I told her I loved her, and always had, but I don't know what my prospects are or what my future holds, and I could not expect her to share in such uncertainty."

"Then let me put your mind at ease. Should both marriages occur, your mother would deed the Bar-M to you. I intend to send my daughter with a dowry of a couple hundred of my best breeding stock. That should be an amiable solution to the other problem, should it not?"

Jay studied the older man's face. "Has Momma told you about our little experiment out there on the range?"

"Experiment?"

Jay smiled. "When you paid for the dead sheep, she used the money to buy calves. We're been running them right in with the sheep up in the hills."

"Cattle and sheep together?" he snorted. "Preposterous."

"They seem to get along fine together. Wouldn't a second 'cash crop' sound good to you when the beef market is down, Colonel? How about the chance to eat a little mutton now and then for something different? Doesn't it even bear thinking about?"

"Hmm, maybe it does. I think I'd like to ride out and see this miracle."

"That's all I ask. And if you are being straight with me on what would happen in this merger, I give you my blessings to marry my mother. And I'd like to ask for your daughter's hand in marriage."

"Gladly, my boy. Looks like we need to get back in touch with that preacher."

Thirty

The colonel is getting married to the sheepherder's mother? Are you sure?" Silbee was upset.

Peyton nodded. "It's all over town."

Silbee threw the curry brush he was using across the barn. "This is a disaster. We have to get rid of the old man before it happens, or else our chances of getting control of that ranch are gone."

"The sheepherder is getting married too."

"To Carrie Sue, no doubt."

"Yup. I think it's going to be a double wedding."

"How touching." He sat down heavily on an anvil.

"That ain't all. That fool Farnsby has gone and got religion."

"You gotta be kidding. Is there a full moon or something? Everything and everybody seems to be going crazy."

"He's telling everybody that will stand still and listen. It's going to be really hard to pin any killings on him. Somebody is going to know where he is all the time if he keeps that up, not to mention the fact that they wouldn't believe he did it."

Silbee threw up his hands. "This is worse than a disaster; it's a total catastrophe. We have to figure out something, and we have to figure it out fast."

Jay and the colonel rode out to the flock. The boys watching the flock eyed the man nervously.

Johnson shook his head in wonder. "I would have never believed it if I wasn't seeing it with my own eyes. They don't seem to mind each other at all."

"That's true, Colonel, and we think they'll grow up to still be that way when they get big."

"Amazing. I find myself wondering if we couldn't contract with you to nursery our calves when they come off their mothers, then take them back off your hands when it's time for them to go into the herd."

Jay hadn't considered that possibility. "That might be a thought. Mixing them with the sheep seems to make them easier to keep an eye on, and shepherds watch over their charges mighty close."

"It just might work."

Silbee and Peyton dismounted on top of the ridge. "What luck!" Silbee said. "There they are together, both of them. We can take care of this problem right now."

Peyton pulled his Winchester. "Wish we had Frank and his sharpshooting rifle with us."

"We don't need him. We have them under our guns. It'll be like shooting ducks in a rain barrel."

Lady's head came up, and she emitted a low growl. "Colonel, we've got company," Jay said quietly.

"Don't be silly. Nobody would dare do anything while I am here with you."

Jay watched the hill Lady seemed to be focused on. He saw a puff of smoke and pushed Johnson hard. It was barely in time as a screaming hornet took Johnson's hat from his head.

"Here now, that was meant for me!" Johnson crawled behind a log, pulling his pistol. Jay dove for his rifle and rolled up behind the same log.

"Welcome to my life," Jay said. "I get this all the time. If I had a dollar for every time Lady has saved my bacon, I'd be richer than you are."

Jay sighted on the hill where the shots had come from and squeezed off several shots, spacing them out.

He was wasting his time. As former rebel soldiers, they changed their firing positions right after they fired a volley.

"I guess they're gone," Jay said.

"Don't be silly." Johnson peeked over the log. "If that's who I think it is, they are well-trained cavalry troops, which means they're trying to flank us right now."

Jay nodded. "I'd say you're right. Lady is trying to bark at two places at once."

"I certainly could have used her in the war."

Jay was out of his element here. "How do you counter-act this here flanking thing, Colonel?"

"Harrumph, well, my favorite strategy would be to have my cavalry sweep through and turn back their flank-ing maneuver on one side, while repositioning my infantry to meet the new threat."

"I forget, Colonel, am I the cavalry or the infantry?"

"That depends. Can you get to your horse without get-ting yourself killed? Your mother would never forgive me if I lost you in battle."

"I think so."

"Then I hereby give you a field commission to brevet major and put you in command of my cavalry."

Jay saluted. "Do I get a sword or something?"

"See me about that later."

"All right, if there is a later."

Jay jumped up and made a dash for his horse, vaulting into the saddle and spurring for the tree line. Bullets hummed around him from two directions.

"The bullets are coming from only two directions," the colonel shouted at his back. "That means there are only two of them or they would have left somebody in front of us."

Jay leaned low over his horse's neck and rode hard and fast. "That boy would have made a fine cavalry trooper," the colonel mused. Then he shifted position to get the log between him and the puffs of smoke he had seen on that side. This movement put the other flanker directly behind him. He had to trust that one to Jay.

He realized that he was putting his life in the hands of a sheepherder, a sheepherder who up until yesterday thought he was trying to kill him. Johnson fervently hoped Jay now thought they were on the same side.

A couple of shots clipped splinters from the log above his head. He was effectively pinned down. Jay was out of sight in the trees.

Jay rode at breakneck speed, too fast to be dodging trees right and left, but it couldn't be helped. Down below he could see the colonel ducking as someone opened up on him from the other side too. He would be dead in less than a minute if ...?

Jay saw the man ahead of him, but the man saw him closing at the same time. He spun to fire at Jay as he came in, but a small brown and white dog hit him solidly in the chest. The rifle he was carrying fired into the air as he tried to protect himself. Seconds later Jay jumped from the horse and landed right in the middle of him.

He recognized the man as Hank Peyton before he left the horse. The colonel had been right.

The two of them rolled down the hill, biting and gouging. Close to the edge of the tree line they ended up against separate tree trunks and quickly scrambled to their feet. Peyton came up with a knife and began to advance.

"I've had it up to here with you, sheep man. I'm going to carve you up and leave you for the buzzards."

"I don't guess it matters to you that I don't have a knife?"

"Of course it matters to me. I'd be much more cautious if you did."

Neither man had a pistol in his holster. Rolling down a hill had that effect unless there was a thong on the hammer to hold the weapon in place, and sometimes even that didn't help.

Taking his eyes off his opponent for split seconds at a time, Jay looked for a stick or a club to use for a weapon. But he already had a weapon, and she hit Peyton again without warning, sinking her teeth into his arm. Jay closed fast.

Just before Jay got to him, Peyton slung Lady off, and she hit a tree hard. She lay still at the bottom. Jay hit him with a punch that had all of his momentum coming down the hill behind it.

"You do really good on dogs; let's see how you are with men," Jay said to the prostrate gunman.

"I'll let you know if I see one," Peyton countered, getting to his feet. "All I see is a sheepherding boy."

"Look while you can, because I intend to close your eyes where you can't even see that."

Peyton swung a punch intended to take Jay's head off, but Jay ducked under it and landed three jarring punches to the ribs of the bigger man. When Peyton dropped an elbow to protect his ribs, Jay swung a wicked short jab over the top, catching Peyton in the mouth and driving him back.

Peyton had concern in his eyes. He hadn't expected to be pressed so hard. Jay followed the punch in, and Peyton landed one on his forehead. That stopped his momentum, but Jay counterpunched so quickly that it kept the big man off balance, making him stagger back a couple of steps. Peyton caught his foot on a rock and went down hard.

Jay jumped on him to follow up on the advantage. Peyton didn't even try to fend him off. He had a shocked look on his face, and bloody spittle came from between his lips. Jay looked at him in puzzlement. Then came a death rattle. Jay turned him over to see that he had fallen back on a jagged tree stump. Peyton was dead.

By the time Jay got up to see about Lady, she was moving, but not too spryly. Jay caught his horse to go check on the colonel and was about to mount when someone threw a shot at him from the top of the hill. Jay could see the shooter; it was Silbee.

Pulling his rifle, he returned fire, and Silbee turned and rode off.

The colonel was on his feet by the time Jay got down to him. "You get a look at them?"

"Peyton is dead up there on the hill. Silbee took a shot at me but missed."

"I was afraid while you were tied up that he would charge me here, but I guess it wasn't his style. I guess it's true he had aspirations about getting rid of me and taking over the Circle J."

"I'd say there's no doubt about that. Lemme go catch your horse, and I'll be right back."

By the time Jay and the colonel got over to the Circle J, Silbee and his two remaining cohorts had gathered their gear and cleared out. "I guess they know that we're on to them," Johnson said. "No matter. Let's go report this to our new sheriff and see if we can make some arrangements with the preacher before he decides it's time to move on again."

Thirty-one

A double wedding? That's great! I've never done one, particularly parents and their children."

"You're so happy about it, you'd think we were just doing this for your entertainment," Jay grinned.

"Well, I couldn't be any happier if you were, but I assure you my happiness is for all of you."

The tent had filled to capacity, and everyone was in their seats. Jay stood at one side of the front, Blake Johnson on the other.

Judy began playing the strains of the wedding march. Instead of asking someone else to give them away, Audrey and Carrie Sue had decided to come down the aisle together. They were beautiful. Carrie was radiant in her white dress and veil, Audrey no less so in her simple yellow dress and matching bonnet. They carried bouquets of Mrs. Tabor's prize roses.

The crowd oh'd and ah'd as the two brides made their way down the aisle.

As they approached the front, the grooms removed their hats and left them off, holding them in hands crossed in front of them. Amos moved to his place in front of the foursome, ready to play his part.

"Ladies," he began, then looked at the men and continued, "gentlemen. We're gathered here in the sight of God and this company in order to create not one family, but two, and hopefully to put an end to a range war at the same time. How could it get any better than that?"

Men all over the audience jumped to their feet shouting and protesting. One of the louder ones cried out, "Say it ain't so, Colonel."

Johnson turned and held up a hand. "Gentlemen, you are ruining what should be one of the most memorable times of our lives." Then he smiled and added "Besides, this isn't even the part where the preacher asks if there's anybody who objects."

He took Audrey's arm in his and spoke softly. "But maybe it's best to speak of this now and put it to rest so we can get on with the ceremony."

He turned around to face the crowd and held up a hand to silence them. "It is true I no longer feel the same way about the sheep."

There was more grumbling and yelling.

He waited it out.

He raised his voice until it rivaled Amos's preaching. "Up in those hills there is a bunch of critters grazing together with no thought of all the yelling and protesting that we are doing; sheep and calves grazing together without a care in the world. Now I'm not saying I want to turn my land over to a bunch of sheep, but I do want to see more of this experiment and learn more about the implications it might have for us all."

He gave a firm look around the room. "My soon-to-be son-in-law asked me if I wouldn't like to diversify a little against those times when the cattle market is soft, or if I wouldn't like to have a little mutton to eat when I get tired of eating beef all the time."

He shrugged. "Those are interesting thoughts, gentlemen, and while I have not made up my mind on them, I want to know more about them. I think we should put off any disagreement on the matter until we ride up there and take a look and talk about the ramifications of what we might see when we get there. Is that asking too much?"

The noise subsided. He stood waiting for more protests, then deciding they were through, turned back around.

Amos said, "I suppose there's no need in asking if there is any objection now when we get to that part of the ceremony." Opening the Bible, he went on with the ceremony. "In Matthew, chapter nineteen, verses five and six, the Lord says this: 'For this cause shall a man leave father and mother, and shall cleave to his wife: and they twain shall be one flesh? Wherefore, they are no more twain, but one flesh. What therefore God hath joined together, let not man put asunder.'"

Amos quit reading, closed the Bible, and looked earnestly at the couples. "In this case it is more than a man and a woman becoming one flesh; it is also a new family being formed where one did not exist before. I charge you to take that responsibility seriously, not only to your spouses, but to the larger family you now find yourself a part of."

He smiled. "Let me put it in terms we can all relate to. We've all seen many a good cowboy make a fast run, and a good throw, only to lose out because he didn't tie the calf with a good knot. I'm here to tell you that when God ties the knot, it's solid."

There were smiles on everyone's faces as he continued. "Ladies, will you promise to love honor and obey these men, to cleave unto them and only them until death do you part?" They both said they did.

Amos turned his attention to the men. "Gentlemen, will you promise to keep, protect, and cherish these ladies, to cleave unto them and only them until death do you part?" They both said they did

"Reckon we can have the rings?"

The rings were produced and given to the couples, who then placed them on their partners' fingers. Then both couples clasped hands. Amos cleared his throat, took his lapels in his hands, and said, "Since both couples have said your I do's and swapped rings, then by the power vested in me I declare you legally and forever hitched in the eyes of God and this assembly."

He leaned forward and winked at them. "Gentlemen, it's right about now I usually point out the fact that you've got some kissing to do."

At the reception after the ceremony, men still had questions, but with the colonel throwing his weight behind Jay, there was no anger demonstrated. They were curious now. They hadn't had as long to come to terms with this new concept as Johnson had, but he had started them thinking.

"I have a new outlook on sheep and shepherds," Brother Ron announced. "I've been reading about it in here." He held up a Bible that was so new that it looked as if it had never been opened. "I can't believe I was so wrong."

"You a sheep lover now, Farnsby?" a man asked.

"Let's just say I have a new appreciation for them."

"You take a heap of getting used to, Farnsby," said Walton. "It's like somebody stole the body of the man you used to be and left this peace-loving Bible-toter in his place."

"Funny you should say that. That's exactly what happened. But I'm not very good at it yet. I read in this Bible every spare minute I have. There's so much I want to learn and understand. I've been spending time with Amos and Joseph, and they are really opening my eyes. But it's a funny thing; I want it all, right now. I want to understand all the things I don't; it's like a hunger."

"Like I say, it takes a heap of getting used to."

Thirty-two

*R*afe, hadn't we better be getting plumb out of here?"
Williams was worried, and he didn't understand why
Silbee wasn't.

"You never were very cool under fire," Silbee said. "If
one battle plan goes awry, the good commander always
has a secondary plan to fall back on."

Williams just didn't get it. "But there ain't nothing here
for us now. No way the colonel is going to cut his daughter out of his will now, and there's a wife to consider too."

"They'll have to all four disappear. Then the Circle J
will belong to whoever is strong enough to take it and hold
it."

"I don't hold with killing womenfolk," Carter said.

Silbee's face was hard as he glared at the man. "It
ain't no different than killing men. You just center that

front sight and pull that trigger. The bullet don't know the difference."

Carter shook his head. "I don't think I can do it."

"If you can't do what I need you to do, then what good are you?" Rage came into Silbee's face instantly, dark and menacing.

"Now wait. I ain't bucking you, Rafe. I just don't know if I have it in me."

"You'll have it in you when the time comes or I'll turn that gun on you."

Carter gulped. There was no way he wanted to get crossways with Silbee. The man was dangerous, and the more his plans went awry, the more unpredictable he became.

Wagons ran both ways as the belongings of Audrey were moved to the big house on the Circle J, and those of Carrie Sue were moved permanently out to the Bar-M.

Jay watched in amazement as his little place began to look less like his mother and more like Carrie Sue. He had never realized how much a house took on the personality of the woman into whose care it fell.

Dishes sat on shelves, pieces of furniture disappeared and were replaced by others foreign to him. Curtains came down and went up, as did wall hangings and pictures. It caused him to realize that his mother really had moved out more surely than watching her drive off in the buggy with Blake, waving and smiling.

Blake. That was going to take some getting used to. Colonel or Mr. Johnson wouldn't do, and, of course, Daddy or Father was out. So Blake it was.

On the other end of the move, the same thing was happening. Blake had retreated to his study, and Esmeralda and Audrey were having a field day putting her stamp on the big house. They had asked Carrie Sue if she would like Esmeralda there with her, but she had said the house wasn't big enough to justify a maid. Then in the next breath she had said she would love for Esmeralda to come to tea occasionally, but as a friend, not a servant.

Audrey took to the role of mistress of the house as if she had been born to it. She was not demanding of those who worked in the house and was much more inclined to do things *with* them instead of issuing instructions *to* them. But when Blake indicated that he would let them go if they weren't needed, she realized that the last thing she wanted to do was cost them their jobs.

It looked for all the world like a sheriff's posse, but that group was over in an entirely different part of the county, combing the countryside for Silbee and his men. This was a group of ranchers and townspeople who had come out to see the miracle of the sheep and the calves.

"Can you beat that?" Judge Willoughby said.

The sheep and calves were spread across the meadow, no longer even divided up into groups.

"It was Mother's idea," Jay explained. "She said cattle and sheep wouldn't mix, everybody was right about that, but she thought it was mostly because the cattle were so big. Plus she said most behavior is learned, whether it's animals or people, and the calves just needed to learn that sheep were all right to be around."

"It's amazing," Walton said.

The colonel said, "What I had in mind to try was to contract with Jay to nursery my young calves as they come off their mothers, then take them back when they are ready to go to the herd. These young men he has watching them give much closer attention than we can give on the ranch. In return for reducing my losses on calves that don't make it, I intend to pay him with a percentage of those calves that survive, only they will be branded with the Bar-M brand and will run with my herd."

"That's an interesting idea, Blake," a rancher said. "And will you end up with an interest in the sheep as well?"

"I'm not opposed to the idea, although I'm not sure on what basis. I do know the missus surprised me with lamb chops last night, and I found them most agreeable."

"That's only fair, Colonel," Jay said, "because that steak I had last night had a funny mark on it that might have been your brand."

"Colonel? I thought—"

"I'm sorry, sir. I'm still working on the Blake part."

"I certainly hope so, because I found the transition from calling you sheepherder to calling you Jay to be an easy one."

Everyone in the group laughed heartily as they moved to the next stop on the tour. They admired the way Paco and his youngsters used the barn as an animal hospital to tend to those animals not doing as well as the others.

"This is yet another reason I think my high losses in calves that don't live through to maturity are going to change with my new plan," said Johnson. "I'm quite sure this is going to be beneficial."

Several others seemed to think the idea had merit. The range war did seem to be over just as Amos had predicted, without a shot having been fired to conclude it.

Thirty-three

S o this is where Farnsby managed to hide out so well."
Silbee kicked aside debris to walk into the little cabin.

Williams made a face at the stench as he entered. "What
a dump."

Carter saw the possibilities. "It'll be all right when we
shovel it out a little, and air it out. If we couldn't find him
here, they won't be able to find us."

Silbee nodded. "I agree. Let's see if we can make this
place livable."

Williams started loading refuse into a box to carry it out,
but he wasn't pleased. "I don't know why we're stopping this
close. We done busted our britches around here. Ain't no
way you're gonna get hold of that ranch now."

"I've already explained that to you. I got nothing standing in my way but an old military has-been, a sheepherder,

and a couple of women. With them out of the way, this valley will belong to whoever is big enough to take it. Anybody got any doubt that 'whoever' is me?"

Williams shook his head, but he wasn't easy in his mind. Sure, he'd heard it before, and it didn't sound any better then than it did now.

"I don't see the three of us getting it done," Carter said cautiously.

"No," Silbee said, "for once I agree with you. I've got a nice little nest egg I've stolen off the old fool over the years, and I intend to do a little recruiting over in Prospect. It won't take many gun hands to make the difference, the way I figure it. I'll be back with them in a couple of days."

Williams's dark eyebrows closed to become a single line. "You going now?"

"No time like the present."

"I kinda figured you might help us straighten the place up."

Silbee spun on him, his face dark. "What are you trying to say?"

I'm not trying to say anything; I got it said, Williams thought. "Nothing, whoever heard of a sergeant-major pulling cleanup duty?"

"You're pushing your luck."

Brother Ron passed the collection plate at services. He spent every spare moment reading the Bible and quizzing Amos, Joseph, or Judy on what he had read. He had a hunger to learn that none of them had seen before.

He had given his testimony to everyone in town. Many were very pleased by the transformation and enjoyed seeing the fruit of it. Some were annoyed beyond belief.

"I don't get it," Brother Ron said to Amos. "Most of my

old friends avoid me like I got the plague or something."

"Why do you think that is?"

"I guess the type folks I was running with are still in the Devil's clutches. But they are the ones that need to hear the message more than anybody."

Amos smiled. He remembered so clearly when he had gone through the same thing with Joseph guiding him. "That's what's frustrating about trying to do the Lord's work. The ones who need it the most are the ones who resist it the hardest."

"Why is that?"

Amos studied his protégé's face. "What did it feel like when God started working on you?"

"Uncomfortable, as if I had something alive gnawing at my stomach."

"There you go. When God puts us under conviction it can really work on us. The more we resist, the more uncomfortable it becomes."

"So it isn't me making them uncomfortable?"

"You are keeping it in front of them, making it happen, but actually it is the Holy Spirit that's really working on them."

"Well, it's for their own good."

"It is indeed."

"You don't mind me constantly asking you this stuff, do you?"

"Not at all. I remember the excitement and hunger of being a new Christian. I wish we could always keep that level of passion for our faith. That's why we have revivals, to try to help us get the fire back when it cools."

"I can't imagine ever cooling." The sincerity on his face was unmistakable.

Amos smiled patiently. "I know."

Thirty-four

*I*f the war between the cowmen and the sheepherders was over in Three Forks, or seemed to be, it made a definite difference when Silbee used it to hire gunmen in Prospect. When he got back to the cabin he had eight riders with him, and they looked as tough as horseshoe nails.

Williams didn't like the looks of them. "Where are all these yahoos going to sleep?"

Silbee brushed the question aside. "We'll make do. It won't be for long. I brought a packhorse full of food too. Why don't you guys unload it and make us something to eat?"

Carter scowled. "Why us? Those are all new fellows, and we've been with you the whole way. Don't we rate wearing some stripes in this outfit?"

"I'm too tired to argue with you. We've been riding all day. Just do what I told you to do."

Carter and Williams grumbled as they started unloading the pack animal. The new men cared for their mounts and turned them into the corral. Then they began to get coffee and settle around the clearing, leaning up against their saddles. One of them held up the pot and said, "Coffee's gone."

"Well, make some more," Carter snarled. "I ain't your mother."

"Ain't you the cook?"

"We ain't got no cook; we just kind of fend for ourselves."

The man seemed to change his mind about the coffee. "What kind of outfit is it that ain't got no cook?" he grumbled as he went over to sit with the rest of the group.

Silbee came out of the cabin. He sat on a stump by the fire and looked at them. He glanced over at Carter and said, "Pour me a cup of coffee."

"Coffee's gone."

"Well, make some more. Do I have to tell you every little thing?"

Carter groused under his breath as he went into the cabin to get some coffee. "Maybe this outfit has a cook after all," he muttered. "I sure didn't sign on to do that."

As Carter put the coffee on to boil, Silbee laid it out for the men. "We've tried being subtle about this, and it didn't work. The way I look at it, it's guerilla warfare now. We're going to raid fast, hit hard, and ride out before anybody can mount a counterattack."

"Sounds like the army to me," a man said.

"That's how we're going to run it, as if we were a military unit," Silbee said. "Anybody got a problem with that?"

"I guess not. I just thought I was through with all that stuff. We ain't gonna have to salute or anything, are we?"

"No, but I will expect everybody to obey orders, and do it without question."

The man glowered. "Or what?"

"Or you won't live to hear another order."

Williams and Carter rode out in the early morning hours. "He's gone around the bend of the river," Carter said.

Williams agreed. "That's one trip I don't want to make with him."

"It'd be different if he didn't treat us like hired help. We rode with him through the whole war. We deserve better."

Williams nodded. "You got any idea where we're going?"

"No, to tell you the truth, I haven't had to think for myself for so long I'm not sure I remember how." Carter gave his saddle mate a sheepish look.

"Ain't it the truth? I'll tell you one thing though. I don't relish leaving out of here with a price on my head."

"Why would there be a price on our heads? We ain't done nothing."

"Well, I did shoot that there deputy," Williams admitted.

"No, you didn't. You tried to shoot the sheriff. The deputy committed suicide by stepping in front of the bullet."

"I guess you're right at that."

"How about we go tell the sheriff we're leaving, tell him that whatever is about to happen we have no part in it, and everything that's happened so far has been Silbee and not us?"

"I like all of that but telling it to the sheriff." Williams still didn't want any part of the law.

"How about we tell it to that ex-sheriff then? He couldn't arrest us, and he'd go make sure everybody knew we was lighting a shuck out of here and why."

"That's better. You really think that deputy committed suicide?"

"No other way to look at it."

Thirty-five

Brother Ron sat reading his Bible under the lantern in the passenger area of the Wells Fargo office when Carter and Williams walked up to him.

Carter said, "Hey, sheriff."

He looked up, a pleasant smile on his face. "I wasn't reelected sheriff, and I'm not the same man I was anyway. I am a new man in Christ now, and people call me Brother Ron."

Carter smiled. "I heard you bought the whole load: wagon, hay, and all. Guess a guy has to see it to believe it."

Williams looked puzzled. "He don't even look like the same guy."

"I assure you," Brother Ron said, "I am most certainly *not* the same guy. What can I do for you gentlemen?"

"We're hauling our freight out of here," Williams said. "We just wanted somebody to know we're going so we won't get blamed for anything that might happen."

Brother Ron frowned. "Is something going to happen you don't want to get blamed for?"

Carter laughed a hollow, mirthless laugh. "Oh yeah, count on it."

"Such as what?" Brother Ron closed the Bible. He sensed an opportunity here, possibly one he was uniquely suited for, being a former lawman who was now a servant of the Lord.

"Silbee has hired him some gun slicks. There's gonna be a bloodbath for sure. We just wanted to make sure folks knew we was gone and had no part in it when it happens."

"Yes, yes, I'll tell the new sheriff. Where is Silbee now? We all thought he had left the country."

Williams shook his head. "He's eat up with the notion of getting rid of the sheepherder and the colonel. Won't listen to reason anymore. We've had enough of him."

"Why aren't you telling this to the sheriff yourself?"

"We ain't done nothing for anybody to blame us for," Carter said. "But we don't want to have to explain it to the law either, just in case somebody sees it some other way."

"So where is Silbee?"

"Out at your old cabin. They're all out there—him and his hired army."

Brother Ron watched as they rode off, then he headed straight for the sheriff's office. As he came in, Cook grimaced and said, "Not now, Farnsby, I ain't in the mood. I'm as happy that you found religion as the next guy, but enough is enough."

"I haven't given up on helping you find peace with the Lord, Danny, but that's not why I'm here."

"So, why are you here?"

"I just talked to Williams and Carter."

"What?" His feet came down with a thud. "I thought that bunch had left the country."

"Everybody thought that, and those two are doing that very thing right now, as fast as their mounts can take them."

"And Silbee?"

"He's got a big burr under his saddle." Brother Ron said. "Williams and Carter said he's set on taking the colonel and Jay down. He thinks that with them out of the way he can take over the whole valley."

"Over my dead body."

"I don't think he'd have a problem with that. He's hired a bunch of gunmen to help him. It's going to get pretty nasty."

"I'm going to have to deputize some more men." Cook pulled a badge out of a drawer and tossed it across the desk to the former sheriff. "Starting with you."

Brother Ron smiled and pushed it back. "I don't believe in violence anymore. I work for a higher authority than the law."

"That book won't protect you from bullets."

"God has protected Christians in a lions' den and in the middle of a fiery furnace; he can protect me here."

Cook looked at him as if his brains were scrambled. "I reckon he could if he said he would, but have you had any promises from him on the subject?"

"I just trust him to do it, and if he doesn't, it's because he has something else in mind."

"I ain't got time for no philosophical debate." Cook put his hat on. "I got to go find me a mess of deputies."

"Yes, you go. Hopefully, they won't be needed."

Cook hurried through the door. He shook his head as he realized that Farnsby probably intended to solve this whole mess with a bunch of prayers. It'd be nice if that was all it took, but he knew it was going to take bullets, not prayers, and plenty of them before this matter was all over and done.

Brother Ron saddled up. He didn't want to see lives lost. He'd trust the protection of the Lord. He headed for his cabin.

The sun was high before he rode into the clearing of his little place. Silbee stood out front. "Well, well, if it isn't the newest angel. What are you doing out here?"

"I had a talk with Williams and Carter."

"Those turncoats! When I get through with all this I'm going to settle with them. What did they tell you? Obviously they told you where I am; what else?"

"They told me of your plans. It was my duty to tell the sheriff, but I don't want to see people getting hurt, so I came out here to talk you into giving up. There's no need for violence here."

"Is that the sheriff or the preacher talking?"

"I'm no longer a sheriff, and I'm not a preacher either. Now I'm just a simple servant of the Lord."

Silbee looked down on his hip. "You came out here without a gun? Are you insane?"

He held up his Bible. "This is all the protection I need."

Without a word, Silbee drew and fired. Brother Ron slumped forward.

"Wasn't much protection, was it?"

Silbee took his hat and slapped his victim's horse on the rump. The animal left the clearing at a dead run.

Thirty-six

Sheriff Cook sent two riders to warn the colonel and Jay. He hoped to head Silbee and his gang off before anything could happen to them, but he didn't want them unprotected in case he failed to do so.

On the edge of town Brother Ron's horse galloped into camp with his unconscious rider slumped over his neck. Amos ran to him, helping him down.

"Is he alive?" Judy asked.

"Seems to still be breathing." Amos answered. He opened Ron's shirt. "Well, look at this."

Judy looked over his shoulder. "Judy, this cross you gave him deflected the bullet. It's in him, but if it hadn't hit this cross first, it'd have hit him dead center in the heart. You'd better go get the doc. Joseph and I will get him over to the wagon."

She ran toward the center of town, skirt and petticoats flying. She met a couple of men and told them what had happened. One of them went for the doctor while the other went in search of the sheriff. She rushed back to camp and put some water on to boil, knowing it would be needed.

The sheriff got there first. "I never dreamed he'd go out there. He said God would protect him. I guess I shoulda realized what he was likely to do."

Amos looked up at the lawman. "You didn't think God would protect him?"

Cook had a guilty look on his face. "I told him I thought God *could*, I just didn't know if he *would* if it wasn't something he had promised to do."

Amos removed the cloth from Ron's chest. "Whether God promised or not, he protected him." He held up the metal cross, disfigured by the impact of the bullet.

Cooks' mouth fell open. "If it hadn't been for that, it would have hit him ..."

Amos smiled. "Yes, right in the heart. Do you have any further thoughts about God's ability to protect his own?"

"Preacher, when I get through with what I've got to do, we need to talk."

"Sheriff, I think the man you need to talk to is lying right here, and unless I miss my guess, he'll be able to do that talking soon enough. I'll be happy to help, but I think he's earned a shot at it, don't you?"

"Maybe you're right."

"We no longer have the luxury of choosing the time," Silbee told his men. "That idiot Farnsby alerted the sheriff. We need to make our move, and we need to make it now."

Sitting around the clearing, the gunmen put fresh cartridges into their rifles and pistols. These were men of action, and they were ready to move.

Silbee paced back and forth. He was in his element, planning a military campaign. He stopped and faced the men, clasped his arms behind his back, and stuck out his chest. "There are only two real threats. First is any men the sheriff can get may come against us. They are sure to have sufficient numbers, but they will be marginal fighters at best. The second threat will be the cowhands at the Circle J. They aren't fighting men either, but they will make a better showing than a bunch of pampered townsmen."

He paused, sorting it out in his head. "The key strategy will be to take advantage of the element of surprise while we have it open to us. If we can wipe out those cowboys while they're at lunch in the cook shed, we can get rid of our largest threat."

He smiled. "That done, we can send the sheriff and his boys packing and then deal with our real objectives at our leisure. Any questions?"

One of the gunmen said, "Aren't we going to be a little shorthanded for this?"

"I thought of that. I sent Clive to town last night to hire some men who recently were part of a group of night riders to add to our numbers."

"Night riders, eh? That'll help."

Silbee resisted a smile. They didn't need to know the quality of the help involved; the night riders were merely recruited to add numbers. He heard horses coming and looked to see a dozen men following Clive into the clearing. He moved to intercept them. He didn't want the two groups to meet and learn more about each other. It would

only disgust his fighting men—and scare the daylights out
of his night riders.

"The sheriff sent me out here to tell you that Silbee
has a bunch of hard cases riding with him. They figure to
wipe out you and the colonel and take over the valley."
Carl's horse was lathered. He had made a hard ride.

Jay was grateful. "I really appreciate it. Is the colonel
being warned?"

Carl nodded. "Another rider is doing that."

"All right, tell them you warned me."

Carl dismounted. "If it's all the same with you, I'll stick
around and lend a hand. They don't need me to report
back."

"You sure about that? You were on the cowmen's side
of this fight. You ready to stand up for a bunch of sheep?"

"No, I'm not. But I'm ready to help you protect your
womenfolk and your home."

Jay laughed. "Fair enough, but I'm not going to protect
this house. I don't have enough guns to make a stand here.
I'm going to have the boys run the flock into the upper valley. If the raiders are silly enough to follow, there's a narrow
pass where we can cut them to ribbons if they try to follow."

"They'll burn your ranch."

"People come first. Houses and barns can be rebuilt,
and speaking of people, a couple of you guys go get Rosita
and the girls loaded up and get them out of there. Take
'em over to the Circle J."

Jason was the other rider, and he gave the same news
to the colonel.

"Silbee is going to ride against me? That scum. He was
my right-hand man. I trusted him above all men."

Then it dawned on him. "Wait a minute. He's going to ride against Jay too?" He buckled on his gun belt and reached for his hat. "I have to go protect my daughter."

"Too late for that, Colonel," Jason said. "If they're riding against them, they're already there, and if it's against you, you'll need everybody you've got."

"Hang it all, I can't sit here and ..."

Johnson fumed for a minute, then thought it through. "You're right, of course. I'll have to trust Jay to take care of her."

He suddenly realized that he couldn't think of any better hands for her to be in. Jay had taken everything he had thrown at him and stood up to it. If anybody could protect Carrie Sue, it would be him.

The sound of gunfire sounded outside. "It looks like we're the primary target," Johnson said. "I should have known. Reduce your most significant threat first. Whatever else he may be, Silbee is a fine military strategist."

Jason grabbed the colonel short of the door. "Don't go out. We can do the others more good from here."

They grabbed rifles and began firing on the raiders. The cook shed was on fire, and good cowboys were being shot as they ran out. The colonel cursed the raiders for the cowards they were.

"They'll be on us in a minute," Jason yelled.

"It'll cost them to cross that yard," Johnson said coolly.

Shots sounded from off to the left, and the raiders broke contact and rode out as Cook and his men rode into the yard. "Looks like we're late," he yelled.

"I'd say in the nick of time, Sheriff," the colonel shouted. "Although you are too late for some good men."

Thirty-seven

A few more minutes, and we'd have had them wiped out." The gunman reloaded his pistol as he talked.

"We did enough," Silbee said. "We took them out of action as a fighting force. Most of them are dead or wounded."

"We go after the sheepherder now?"

"No," Silbee said, "we remove the second threat, the posse."

The gunman removed his hat and wiped his forehead with his shirtsleeve. "They missed a chance; if it'd been me, I'd have stayed after us. They've given us time to regroup."

"Yes, that was a tactical error, not following up their advantage. Where do you figure they'll go now?" Silbee had an idea but wanted to hear a second opinion.

"To protect that sheepherder; that's why I said we ought to go there."

"You're right about their movement, but not on the proper strategy. We need to cut through and position ourselves in the rocks overlooking the trail just before the river crossing. We can look down our rifle barrels at them there."

"Good plan."

"We won't get it done sitting here. Let's ride."

With Carl's help—an unnatural act for the cowboy—they got the flock moved through the narrow pass. "I can't believe these cows will just run right with these critters. I heard about it, but I guess you've gotta see it for it to sink in."

Carl watched Lady funnel them through the opening, shaking his head in awe. "That dog is sort of hard on a cowboy's ego. She's doing a job it'd take four good hands to do."

Jay knew what he meant. "Yes, she's a marvel. I was a cowboy too, you know. My first reaction to her was pretty much the same."

"Hope this doesn't catch on. A few of those dogs could put an awful lot of good cowboys out of work."

"Don't worry about it," Jay said, laughing. "There are still a lot of things a dog can't do that a cowboy can."

"Sure, like gripe and complain. A dog just can't do that."

"There you go."

Lady and the boys took the flock on up the slope. Jay and Carrie Sue settled in on one side of the pass, rifles in hand, while Carl and Paco did the same on the other side. There was nothing to do now but wait.

The posse rode hard toward the Bar-M. The men in it were high on their success with the initial contact with the raiders. They were eager to run them to ground. They rounded the rocks headed for the stream crossing when the rifles opened up above them.

Several saddles emptied immediately. The rest of the posse dove for the ground and took shelter behind some live oak trees where they returned fire.

The rifles on the hill were deadly accurate, those below mostly ineffective. More men were wounded in the ranks of the posse.

"Should we flank them and finish them off?" asked one of the gunmen.

Silbee shook his head. "No, I have to live here after this is all over. I want them afraid of me, but not to the point where I can't get along with them. Take two men and run off their horses. That'll take them out of action for the duration of the campaign, particularly by the time they get aid for their wounded. We'll take out the sheepherder next."

They mounted and headed for the Bar-M. Pausing just within sight of the ranch, Silbee split his forces in half, then swept into the ranch from two sides at once. They fired at everything in sight, but it was several minutes before they figured out that the place was deserted.

Silbee looked disgusted. "I keep underestimating that sheepherder. Who would have guessed he wouldn't make his stand here at the ranch?"

The men spread out and searched, but they came up empty-handed. Silbee was furious.

"Torch it," he said as he turned and rode off.

From the pass, the column of smoke in the distance was unmistakable. "They've fired the house," Jay said.

"All my pretty things," Carrie Sue said and began to cry. He put his arm around her. There was nothing to be said.

"They'll be here soon," he said. "That flock isn't hard to track. If they destroyed the ranch buildings, they'll want to destroy the flock, too."

These were prophetic words. Down below Silbee saw the imprint of a thousand little pointed hooves. "I don't need a tracker to do this, do I?"

"I'm going to enjoy this part," one of the men said. "I hate them little fuzzy critters."

"It's what I signed on for," another agreed.

They were able to follow the trail at a steady trot. They had turned up the slope toward a narrow pass when Silbee pulled up.

"They went up that way for sure," a night rider said.

This was a better ambush site than the one Silbee had used on the posse, and he recognized it immediately. This is what he had brought the night riders for. He named one to be in charge and told him to track the group up the slope while he and the remaining men flanked them. The group didn't seem to realize he was using them as decoys for the ambush.

Silbee and his men hadn't even gotten out of sight before they heard the rifles open up. *I should have had them wait to give us time to come around their east flank,* he thought. *It sounds like they are getting shot up so fast that I won't even be able to take advantage of the diversion.*

"It sounds like they've run into something," one of the men said.

"Sounds to me like they're getting shot up," another one added.

"Yes," Silbee said, "we've lost the element of surprise. We'd better break off this engagement and regroup."

Thirty-eight

*I*t hadn't been anywhere near the massacre Silbee had imagined. Faced by a withering barrage of fire, the night riders went to ground and covered up like prairie dogs caught in a hailstorm. Handkerchiefs, bandannas, and cloths of every imaginable size and description fluttered all over the floor of the pass.

Jay laughed. "It's Farnsby's Raiders." He yelled for them to throw down their weapons, and they came sailing across like a meteor shower.

He got up to go down and gather up the weapons. "Watch for Silbee," he said to Carrie Sue. "He has to be around here somewhere."

"You be careful," she said.

"There's nothing to fear from these clowns. Just don't let Silbee sneak up on me."

The men all held their hands high as he walked up to them. "You boys look a mite naked without your flour sacks on."

"I'm giving up the night-riding business," one man whined. "It goes bad for us every time we try it."

"I could use another shepherd," Jay said with a grin.

"No kidding?" the man said eagerly. "I think I might could do that."

There was a chorus of belligerent yells, but the man looked as if it was something he'd really like to talk more about.

"We'll talk about that later," Jay said. "Where's Silbee?"

"He sent us this way, and he took some other men and said he was going to flank you."

Paco had gone higher for a look, and Jay saw him returning. "See anything?" he asked.

"*Sí*, Señor, they were crossing the valley headed north. They will not be back today, I think."

"How many did you see?"

"I counted nine, Señor."

Jay looked at the cowering men. "That about right?"

They all nodded vigorously.

"One last question: Where is he hiding out?"

They were fully cooperative now and gave detailed directions to the cabin back up in the hills.

"All right, since you've been so helpful, I'm going to take pity on you boys. Shuck out of your pants and boots."

Another chorus of shouts erupted, but they were silenced immediately when Jay cocked his rifle. Quickly they began to do as he said.

"Now you boys head on back to town. I figure by the time you get there you'll be so footsore that you won't be up to any more mischief for a few days. But if you do, I have to warn you that I'm shooting you on sight if you ever come up against me again. Do I make myself clear?"

He got a rousing affirmation on that one.

"If you play your cards right and are really lucky, you *might* be able to catch one of your horses. Then you *might* be able to use that one to catch the others. Otherwise, you're in for one really long walk."

Johnson was fit to be tied. "I can't wait any longer. I have to go see about Carrie Sue."

"Not without me, Blake," Audrey said.

"It's too dangerous." He put his foot down, knowing full well that there had never been a time in his life when any woman had ever done what he told her to do.

They saddled up and rode out, accompanied by three cowboys still in good enough condition to ride. Their hearts sank as they got close enough to the Bar-M to see the smoking, burned-out buildings. There were no signs of life.

"It's worse than I thought," Blake said.

"Don't give up so easy," Audrey said resolutely. "I know my son. He'd never allow himself to be trapped this way."

"You're right, I wouldn't let that happen," a voice sounded behind them.

They turned to see Jay enter the clearing, leading his horse. Carrie Sue was mounted coming in behind him. The colonel was breathing deeply, trying to recover from the emotions that had just taken him on such a violent ride. "I thought I'd lost you," he said to Carrie Sue.

"I'm fine. I was with Jay."

"Where's Paco?" Audrey asked anxiously.

"He's all right; he and Carl are with the sheep. He wanted me to check on his family though."

"They're fine. They're at the ranch."

"I was sure worried, then I was surprised to discover that I felt yours were the most competent hands for her to be in," Johnson said to Jay. "I admit, I just got through wondering if I had been correct in that assessment when I saw your ranch. I'm pleased you turned out to be exactly the man I thought you were." He stepped over and offered his hand.

Jay took it. "Thank you, sir."

"I'm sorry about your place though. Too bad."

"It's just buildings. They can be rebuilt. I figured it was better to protect the people."

"As you should have. In my case we defended the ranch, and it is safe. Yet it is not worth the cost. I wish I had sacrificed the buildings and saved the cowboys as you did."

Audrey scolded him. "That's not fair, Blake. The gunmen surprised you. You didn't even have the opportunity to make that decision."

"I suppose not."

Thirty-nine

*J*ay and Carrie Sue returned with Blake and Audrey to the Circle J where they found Sheriff Cook and his deputies. They had converted the bunkhouse into a hospital with the wounded from both groups. Cook said, "I sent a man for the doctor."

"How bad is it?" Blake asked.

"Most of them will be all right in time," Cook said. "A couple are pretty bad. We lost two."

"Actually I'm relieved. I thought it was much worse."

"I don't think they wanted to kill unless they had to. I think they just wanted them out of action."

"That would make sense. Silbee is a very practical man. If he expected to take over the valley, he would not want feelings running so high that he could not repair them in time."

"They caught us cold. I don't think we hit a one of them."

Blake nodded. "The same here, complete tactical surprise. I don't think they suffered a single casualty."

"Take heart, boys," Jay said. "We reduced their force by better than half out at our place."

Blake threw back his head and laughed.

"What's so funny?" asked Cook.

"You don't see the humor? A career military officer and a professional lawman, and we are both bested by a sheepherder."

"I guess we were at that."

Blake's laughter subsided. "Ah well, if the force arrayed against us is unimpaired, diminished by the loss of the night riders, of course," he gave a small bow to Jay, who acknowledged it, "then we may expect further actions. We had best prepare a battle plan."

"I agree," Cook said.

"I wonder what their strength is." Blake looked at Jay.

"Paco saw nine men counting Silbee ride away from our little surprise party."

"Not nine men, but nine battle-hardened veterans," Blake corrected. "And we are three."

"Paco and Carl are out with the sheep. They're fit to fight."

"Who is Carl?" Johnson asked.

"He's a cowboy that was passing through looking for work," Cook said. "He volunteered to take the word out to the Bar-M."

Blake said, "If he's looking for work, I appear to have something to offer him."

Jay smiled. "Actually, I think he's developed something of a liking for sheep, much to his surprise."

"It appears to be catching on. Very well, that's five, and I have three cowboys fit enough to help. No, wait, one went to town for the doctor."

"He's back now." They turned to see Brother Amos enter and say, "Doc is out treating the wounded now. They also brought one rather unusual gun-toting preacher with them."

"We couldn't let you get involved, Preacher," Jay said.

"It isn't up to you, I fear. God gets involved on the side of the righteous, and sometimes that entails his servants taking up arms at his direction and under his protection."

"Nine against nine," Cook said.

Blake nodded. "It appears to be."

Audrey watched the men huddle across the room. "I can't stand this."

Carrie Sue put an arm on her shoulder. "I'm used to being in the family of a warrior. I watched Daddy ride off to do battle my whole life. He always came back, but I never knew if he would. I just had to trust—in him, and in God."

"That's easier to say than to do."

Carrie Sue smiled. "Of course it is. What in life isn't easier to say than to do? It's always been women's place to sit and wait, and suffer in our own quiet way."

"I'd rather take a gun and go with them."

"I would too, but there comes a time when we have to let them do it, and this is that time."

Audrey put a hand on the younger woman's face. "So young, yet so wise."

"It isn't a matter of age, but of experience."

"Our scout came back," Silbee said. "Both of our intended targets are together at the Circle J."

"Yeah," the gunman confirmed, "there are a lot of men there, but most of them are out of business."

"Unacceptable risk," Silbee said. "I can't tell you how many times I've seen badly wounded men get up when they heard the sounds of battle and give amazing accounts of themselves. No, we gotta get our targets away from the ranch where that can't happen." He smiled. "And to minimize damage to my future ranch."

"How are we gonna do that?"

"I don't believe it'll be a problem. They're going to be thinking exactly the same way. They have womenfolk and wounded there at the Circle J and will choose to meet us somewhere off the property. We'll allow them to make that choice, but the actual site of the conflict, you may be sure, will be of *my* choosing."

Dawn was a gray light in the eastern sky. The air was chilled, and bones were stiff as they mounted. The horses stamped their feet in protest of having to be out of the comparative warmth of the barn. Audrey and Carrie Sue looked up at their men. They felt an intense pride and overwhelming dread, all at the same time.

"I don't like this, Blake," Audrey said.

Blake smiled. "It isn't of my choosing, but it has to be done."

"How can you go up against professional gunmen? None of you are gunfighters."

"We have right on our side, dear. The parson is visible evidence of that."

Next to them, Carrie Sue clung to Jay's leg as he sat on his horse. "Please let me go. I'm as good a shot with a rifle as any man here."

"You can't ask me to do that. There comes a time when a man has to stand and protect those he loves. Now is that time."

"If I might suggest," Amos said to Carrie, "the help we need the most, you are in a position to help provide."

Carrie Sue looked up at him. "Prayer?"

He smiled. "I spent an entire hour on my knees this morning, but I wouldn't object to you two continuing to go to the Lord on our behalf."

"Yes, of course we will," said Audrey.

With that the men turned and rode double file out the ranch gate, under the swinging Circle J emblem, which was moving slightly in the early morning breeze. Blake looked up at his brand and wondered if it would soon be changed to the Circle S.

Forty

*T*wo lines of men sat on their horses looking at one another across the expanse of the small valley. The sun now peeked over the horizon, and the low-level rays painted the foliage with unbelievably rich colors. Battle was often like that: terrible events set against beautiful scenic backgrounds.

"Gentlemen," Amos said, "I think one last appeal to our Creator is in order."

They agreed and removed their hats.

"Heavenly Father, we come to you this morning asking for your help and protection. We don't go up against these men with malice in our hearts, but in defense of our homes and loved ones. We claim your love and protection. We recognize that these men kill for a living. We are under no illusions about our chances if we are not protected by your power. Like David before Goliath, we put ourselves in your hands and ask that you empower us to deal with the giant that opposes us. We ask these things in Jesus' name, amen."

Jay had a smile on his face as they put their hats back on.

"I say something funny?" Amos asked.

"No, it was just that I told my shepherds the story about David and Goliath just the other day. As shepherds, they related to it in a big way. I was just remembering that story."

Amos smiled too. "We would all do well to remember that story now."

Blake had a funny look on his face. "We should remember it indeed. As I recall, King Saul had to send a champion out to meet that giant, and they were to fight to the death—winner take all."

Amos nodded. "That's correct."

"Are you thinking we should offer to do that now?"

He nodded. "I am indeed. I don't want my young cowboys hurt trying to go up against professional gunfighters. I don't want you and the sheriff hurt trying to fight my battles for me."

"It's my fight too," Cook said. "These men are lawbreakers, and things need to be set right."

"I licked Silbee once, and I can do it again," Jay said. "Although I can't say I'm comfortable with the ranch riding on the outcome."

"You would be my David, huh?" said Blake. "I like that, and I have no doubt you could do it, but that isn't what I'm thinking at all. I've always thought King Saul was a coward not to do his own fighting."

"That wasn't God's plan," said Amos.

"I understand that, but he didn't even as much as offer to do it. I think he was a coward, and I intend to do my own fighting."

"You can't go up against Silbee; he'll kill you." Jay now genuinely liked his father-in-law. All of the old animosity was gone.

"You don't understand. If I am to lose all I have worked for, I don't want to be here to see it. And I would like to have the decision of whether I keep it or lose it on my own shoulders."

"You think Silbee will agree to that?" asked Cook.

"I know he will. I think he has a score to settle with me, and this will be his chance to get the ranch 'fair and square' and settle some imagined grudge all at the same time. Preacher, will you be my second and ride forth under a white flag? As the challenged party, the choice of weapons is his."

Amos tied a handkerchief to the barrel of his rifle and rode down the slope.

"What are they doing?" one of the gunmen asked.

Silbee looked at the group on the opposite ridge through a collapsible spyglass. "They're praying," Silbee said, and then laughed. "There seems to be a religious epidemic taking place since that preacher hit town. Sure makes them easy picking."

"One of them is coming this way."

"Yeah, it's that preacher. He's flying a flag of truce. I'll go see what he wants."

He folded the telescope, put it in his saddlebag, and rode down the slope. He pulled up beside Amos in the center of the field.

Silbee glanced down at his hip. "Unusual to see a preacher wearing a gun."

"I haven't always been a preacher."

There was no emotion in Silbee's face, always the consummate soldier. "So what are we here for?"

"Colonel Johnson has challenged you to single combat. He feels it is ridiculous for a bunch of people to kill each other over something that in the final analysis is between the two of you."

That response surprised Silbee, but it pleased him at the same time. "I couldn't agree more, and it gives me the chance to be sure I am the one who gives that old fool what he has coming to him."

"You're entitled to name a second for yourself."

"Out of that scum on the hill? I don't see how I could do better than some goody-goody Bible-toter; you're all right with me."

"Very well," Amos said, "the choice of weapons is yours."

"He's sitting up there expecting it to be hand to hand, maybe hand to hand with knives. That would be too easy. Does he still have his saber in the scabbard on his saddle?"

Amos nodded. "Yes, I saw it as he saddled up."

"Once cavalry, always cavalry. I have mine as well, and that's what I choose. He fancies himself to be proficient with it, but I know that's nothing but bluster as is everything else about him. I intend to kill him with his own preferred weapon."

"A sword, how appropriate. David finished up with a sword."

"David? What are you jabbering about?"

"Nothing. I'll take your pistol and rifle."

"Of course." Silbee handed them over.

"You understand I am required to shoot either of you that pulls a weapon not specified or otherwise breaks the rules?"

"You could do that?"

"If I had to." Amos waved Blake down. He held up Silbee's rifle and pistol, and Blake took off his own weapons and handed them to Jay, then rode down the hill.

As he rode up, the two men looked at one another. "I never thought you'd turn on me this way, Sergeant," Blake said.

"I should have killed you on the battlefield, you pompous old fool. You've been grit in my craw for years."

"Am I to understand it is to be sabers?"

Silbee laughed. "Not what you expected, is it? You expected some man-to-man bravado thing where you would be vindicated if you lost. No such luck. You've always told everybody what a fine swordsman you are. I intend to show you up once and for all and expose you for the blundering spectacle that you have always been."

"Have you hated me so much?"

"More than you could possibly know."

"I always thought I enjoyed your respect," Blake said sadly. "How long has this been going on?"

"You had me fooled at first, but then I saw through you. You postured and gave orders, while other men did your fighting and dying for you. But when all was said and done, we took the bullets, and you took the glory. I'm going to strip all that from you today."

"What is your pleasure, gentlemen?" Amos asked. "Will you fight from horseback, or on the ground?"

"Horseback," both men said in unison.

"Once cavalry, always cavalry," Blake said.

"Exactly," Silbee agreed.

Forty-one

*T*he two men rode to the opposite edges of the clearing and turned to face each other, naked blades held erect against their right shoulders. Amos held a pistol in his hand. He would signal the start of the duel with it, then hold it in readiness to enforce the rules.

On the ridge the mercenary gunmen were just beginning to get the picture. "Them two are going to fight it out instead of us fighting?" one of them asked.

"That seems to be the case," another responded.

"This is good. This is very good."

"How do you see it?"

"Silbee's sure to take that old man, but supposing he doesn't?" said the first man. "If he figured the strongest man could take that ranch with the old man dead, we could still make that happen."

"He hollered at us not to mix into it."

"But if he loses, he won't be giving orders anymore, will he?"

"I guess not."

"All right, if Silbee loses, which ain't likely, we ride down on them before they have time to figure out what's going on. Everybody in?" Everyone in the group nodded.

"I don't think you're thinking this through," another man said.

"How's that?"

"Even if Silbee does win, won't he find himself sitting at the bottom of the hill with nothing but a pig-sticker in his hands?"

"With us and them both riding down on him?"

They exchanged wicked grins. "I'm thinking there's gonna be some new kingpins in the valley when all the dust settles."

On the opposite ridge, Cook asked Jay, "Has the old man got a chance?"

"Yeah, I don't know why Silbee chose to do it this way, but Blake has a better chance with a sword than any other weapon he might have picked."

"Maybe he wanted it to be clean and aboveboard so he could hold his head up in the valley when he took over the ranch," Cook suggested.

"Reckon he might have been thinking that way, or maybe he just figured that was the way that'd humiliate Blake the most. Do you think those men up on the hill will stay out of it if Blake wins?"

"Not a chance."

"That's what I thought. We'd best have our rifles out and ready."

Amos fired the shot that sent the two riders toward each other, bending low over their horses' necks, sabers extended out in front. They spurred their mounts to a full gallop and reached out for one other as if with giant, probing fingers.

Silbee's blade skittered along Blake's side, and he winced, immediately reining his horse to a sliding stop. Silbee did the same. They reined around tightly, now close to each other.

"I see I drew first blood," Silbee said, nodding at the cut on Blake's side. The sabers went high over their heads, and they closed the distance, hacking at each other, blades flashing in the early morning sun. Blake parried a hacking blow and slid off to the side to follow it up with a slashing horizontal cut.

It opened a slit in the front of Silbee's shirt, which began to seep red.

"That was close." Silbee backed his horse a couple of steps and looked down. "It appears we're even. How about we get down where I can look you in the eyes as I kill you?"

"As you wish." Both men stepped down, warily watching lest the other man fail to follow through and get the advantage.

The horses walked a few steps away and began to graze, unaware of the conduct of the humans that they would have surely found to be ridiculous had they understood it. Silbee did a couple of squats, limbering himself up as if he were about to have a fencing match.

"I'm going to enjoy this," he said with a cool smile.

Blake did no posturing at all, but stood with his blade pointed down, conserving his strength, not giving away what he intended to be his initial strategy.

Silbee came at him, saber extended, with that peculiar kicking step used in a classic fencing attack. Blake parried the thrust aside, slicing behind it, but Silbee jumped back causing the blade to miss, then struck hard down on the blade as he recovered.

He tried to follow it up, but Blake met each blow.

"My, my," Silbee said with a cruel smile. "So you really do have some skill. How delightful. It'll make victory all the sweeter."

Blake continued to stand casually, blade down, giving away nothing of his intent by his movement, his eyes, or his words. He had no intention of engaging in foolish banter.

Silbee attacked with a series of hard, hacking blows intended to drive Blake back down, but the smaller man met them one at a time, giving way slowly, the defense taking every ounce of his strength.

Suddenly he blocked a blow and spun to the side, momentarily turning his back to Silbee. The bigger man glanced at him to see his exposed back right beside his sword hand. He raised his elbow to put his entire weight into a blow aimed at Blake's back, but by the time the blade descended, Blake was no longer there

Blake had finished the spin, sending a slicing blow up under Silbee's raised elbow and deep under his arm.

Silbee dropped to his knees, a stunned look on his face.

"They didn't teach that one in basic training, did they?" Blake said. "You had to go to a real fencing school to learn that maneuver."

Blake reached over and took the blade from the stunned man who was staring dumbly at the blood running profusely down his side. Blake could have administered the *coup de grâce*, the traditional final blow used to end a duel. He didn't do so.

"Can you believe that old codger beat Silbee?" said the man on the hill. "That's our signal, boys; let's go get 'em."

The men began to ride down on Amos and Blake in the valley. As soon as they started to move, Jay and the others rode to meet them.

The dreaded conflict would take place after all. One of the enemy's number had been disabled, but in return two of their own were sitting ducks in the middle of the field. This was going to be bad.

The two groups closed the gap, the air filled with spiteful, spitting bullets. In seconds they would be upon one another.

A volley of shots sounded from the hill, and several charging horses went down. The mercenaries looked to see a body of men riding down on them from the top of the opposing ridge. Two women led the charge. The mercenaries doubled up on remaining horses and fled for their lives.

Both groups met in the center of the field.

"Where did you find all these men?" Jay asked Carrie Sue.

"We gathered up all the cowboys and ranchers from the surrounding spreads."

"For once I'm sure glad you're too bull-headed to do as you're told."

Carrie Sue smiled sweetly. "Someone has to save you men from your pig-headed pride."

"It appears you decided to do something more constructive than praying," said Amos.

"Not at all," Audrey replied, "but women can do more than one thing at a time."

She got down and went to look at Silbee's wound. She began to tear strips from her petticoat. "If I can stop the flow of blood, I believe we can save him."

Silbee looked at her with dazed confusion in his eyes. "Why would you do that?"

"Because it's the right thing to do, just as it was the right thing to do for Blake not to finish you off when he had the chance. I'm so proud of him."

"I would have done it to him."

"Of course you would have; that's what makes him the better man. Now hold your arm up where I can get this wrapped around you."

"Do a good job, ma'am," Sheriff Cook said. "Because I have plans for him. Plans that include territorial prison until he's so old he can't walk without help."

Forty-two

*T*hey were all there for the going-away party. Amos, Judy, and Joseph would be leaving at first light. Blake said, "We all wish you would just stay here with us. We could have a church up in a couple of weeks."

Amos smiled. "I have a home church when I can get back to it, but don't let that stop you from building one. When you have one, God will fill it; I promise you that. As a matter of fact, I think Brother Ron is coming along nicely. He's going to travel with us for a bit, and I think by the time you have your church built, we'll have turned him into a first-class preacher."

"But why do you have to go?" asked Audrey.

"I have to get on to Denver. I did some bad things up there in a former life, and I have to go atone for them."

"I'd say you are counting on the Lord's protection an awful lot," said Jay.

"I am for a fact, and he has been most faithful. I am well aware that physical protection is not something he has promised us. Someday he may allow something else to happen, and I am prepared for that. I explained that to Brother Ron as well. It is not intended that we substitute blind faith for common sense. God expects us to consider the consequences of our actions, unless we are in such a position that we have no alternative but to throw ourselves on his mercy."

"I'm right glad you said that," Jay responded. "I mean, I wasn't comfortable saying anything about it, but I was worried that Ron was counting on protection that was too much to ask. But how do you know? I sure ain't got Bible learning enough to say."

"I think Brother Ron and I reached an understanding on it. I never met a man with as much fire in him to serve the Lord. He's going to make a fine minister."

"Well, everybody knows him here, and they watched him grow into his faith," said Blake. "I think people will take right well to him as their pastor."

"We're going to miss you, Preacher," said Carrie Sue. "Don't forget the way back." She paused for a moment as if she were framing her words. "You know what? When you came here, do you remember what you first preached?"

"On the Great Shepherd."

"Yes, you compared us to a flock of sheep that was dependent on our shepherd. Could you ever have realized how prophetic those words would turn out to be?"

"No, not at all." Amos smiled. "But the One who gave me the words to say knew exactly what he was doing, don't you think?"

READERS' GUIDE

For Personal Reflection
or Group Discussion

Readers' Guide

1. Christians have wrestled with the choice between their faith and their duty for years. How did you feel about Amos picking up a gun and playing an active role in the situation he faced? What would you have done in his situation?

2. Is there ever justification in picking up a sword in defense of home and country as in Old Testament times? Have you ever done so yourself, or would you do so if necessary? Why or why not?

3. How did you feel about the transition of Sheriff Farnsby from shallow egotist to obsessed fanatic, to beaten derelict, and finally to a man of faith every bit as driven as he had been in earlier roles?

4. How vital to the storyline was Farnsby's transition and growth?

5. Did it put you in mind of Paul, who was as dedicated as a Christian as he had been earlier persecuting Christians?

6. This story was about Jay and his mother trying to save their little ranch the only way they knew how—or was it?

7. Was this the main story or merely a plot mechanism to allow us to see the development in the lives of the central characters?

8. Several characters did make dramatic changes over the course of the story. Why didn't Rafe Silbee change for the better?

9. Did he change at all?

10. Do you think it is true that those who have the farthest to come spiritually to find redemption commit to service the strongest, not stopping at being "casual Christians"?

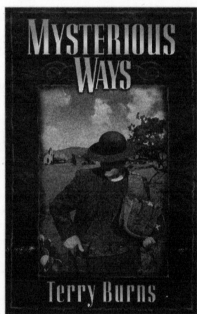

MISTAKEN IDENTITY. ROBBERY. FALSE ARREST. RACE RIOTS.
IT'S JUST ANOTHER DAY IN THE OLD WEST.

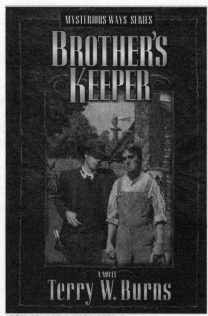

ISBN-13: 978-1-5891-9035-1
ISBN-10: 1-58919-035-1 • Item#: 103816
320 Pages • Paperback • $12.99

Brother's Keeper

James and Ross Campbell are identical twins—and that's where the similarities stop. Ross is an outlaw with a Texas Ranger on his trail; James and his mother run the quiet family farm. But a twist of fate forces them to seek out Ross, accompanied by the lovely Mary Jane McMinn, who gives a new meaning to the term "Calamity Jane." Before long the trio finds more adventure than they ever imagined: crossing the Mississippi, facing false arrest, and meeting up with a certain traveling preacher. When the family comes face-to-face with danger, Ross begins to understand the undeniable bond between twins, the heart of sacrificial love, and the full meaning of being your *Brother's Keeper*.

Additional copies of *Shepherd's Son* are available wherever good books are sold.

If you have enjoyed this book,
or if it has had an impact on your life,
we would like to hear from you.

Please contact us at:

RiverOak Books
Cook Communications Ministries, Dept. 201
4050 Lee Vance View
Colorado Springs, CO 80918
Or
visit our Web site: www.cookministries.com